Lynne Graham

The Billionaire's Bridal Bargain

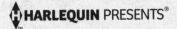
HARLEQUIN PRESENTS®

ISBN-13: 978-0-373-13805-0

The Billionaire's Bridal Bargain

First North American publication 2015

Copyright © 2015 by Lynne Graham

Recycling programs
for this product may
not exist in your area.

Printed in U.S.A.

™ www.Harlequin.com

Cesare turned to look at Lizzie only when she reached the altar. Eyes the color of melted bronze assailed her and she stopped breathing, gripped by the ferocious force of will in that appraisal. He had no doubts, she interpreted. He knew exactly what he was doing, had come to terms with the drawbacks and was concentrating on the endgame.

She had to do the same, Lizzie told herself urgently. She had to stop trying to personalize their relationship and stop wondering whether or not he would kiss her after they had been pronounced man and wife. Such treacherous thoughts were far removed from businesslike behavior and utterly inappropriate, she scolded herself in exasperation.

"You look fantastic," Cesare murmured softly while he threaded the wedding band on to her finger, and she followed suit, copying his maneuver with less cool and more nerves.

Indeed, Cesare was taken aback by just how fabulous she looked. The effect she had on him was ever so slightly unnerving. It was his libido, he told himself impatiently. As long as he stuck to his rules of never getting tangled in anything that smacked of an emotional connection, he would be fine and perfectly happy.

Bound by Gold

Captivated by passion

Lizzie and Chrissie Whitaker: two ordinary girls until they meet two extraordinary men! But these men are renowned for getting what they want... whatever the cost.

Explosive passion and powerful men astound in Lynne Graham's fabulous new duet.

Read Lizzie's story in

The Billionaire's Bridal Bargain

April 2015

Lizzie refuses to marry Cesare Sabatino so he can get his hands on her Mediterranean island inheritance. But no one says no to the formidable tycoon and soon Lizzie is going from "I don't," to "I do!"

Read Chrissie's story in

The Sheikh's Secret Babies

May 2015

Chrissie never told her sister who was the father of her twin babies. When the Prince of Marwan storms back into her life, determined to claim his heirs, Chrissie is forced to recognize him...as her husband!

Lynne Graham was born in Northern Ireland and has been a keen romance reader since her teens. She is very happily married, with an understanding husband who has learned to cook since she started to write. Her five children keep her on her toes. She has a very large dog, which knocks everything over, a very small terrier, which barks a lot, and two cats. When time allows, Lynne is a keen gardener.

Books by Lynne Graham

Harlequin Presents

The Secret His Mistress Carried
The Dimitrakos Proposition
A Ring to Secure His Heir
Unlocking Her Innocence

The Legacies of Powerful Men

Ravelli's Defiant Bride
Christakis's Rebellious Wife
Zarif's Convenient Queen

A Bride for a Billionaire

A Rich Man's Whim
The Sheikh's Prize
The Billionaire's Trophy
Challenging Dante

Visit the Author Profile page
at Harlequin.com for more titles.

CHAPTER ONE

CESARE SABATINO FLIPPED open the file sent by special delivery and groaned out loud, his darkly handsome features betraying his disbelief.

There were two photos included in the file, one of a nubile blonde teenager called Cristina and the other of her older sister Elisabetta. Was this familial insanity to visit yet another generation? Cesare raked long brown fingers through his luxuriant black hair, frustration pumping through every long lean line of his powerful body. He really didn't have time for such nonsense in the middle of his working day. What was his father, Goffredo, playing at?

'What's up?' Jonathan, his friend and a director of the Sabatino pharmaceutical empire, asked.

In answer, Cesare tossed the file to the

other man. 'Look at it and weep at the madness that can afflict even one's seemingly sane relatives,' he urged.

Frowning, Jonathan glanced through the sparse file and studied the photos. 'The blonde's not bad but a bit on the young side. The other one with the woolly hat on looks like a scarecrow. What on earth is the connection between you and some Yorkshire farming family?'

'It's a long story,' Cesare warned him.

Jonathan hitched his well-cut trousers and took a seat. 'Interesting?'

Cesare grimaced. 'Only moderately. In the nineteen thirties my family owned a small island called Lionos in the Aegean Sea. Most of my ancestors on my father's side are buried there. My grandmother, Athene, was born and raised there. But when her father went bust, Lionos was sold to an Italian called Geraldo Luccini.'

Jonathan shrugged. 'Fortunes rise and fall.'

'Matters, however, took a turn for the worse when Athene's brother decided to get the island back into family hands by marrying Luccini's daughter and then chose to jilt her at the altar.'

The other man raised his brows. 'Nice…'

'Her father was so enraged by the slight to his daughter and his family that Lionos was eternally tied up in Geraldo's exceedingly complex will.'

'In what way?'

'The island cannot be sold and the two young women in that file are the current owners of Lionos by inheritance through their mother. The island can only be regained by my family through marriage between a Zirondi and a Luccini descendant and the birth of a child.'

'You're not serious?' Jonathan was amazed.

'A generation back, my father was serious enough to propose marriage to the mother of those two girls, Francesca, although I would point out that he genuinely fell in love with her. Luckily for us all, however, when he proposed she turned him down and married her farmer instead.'

'Why luckily?' Jonathan queried.

'Francesca didn't settle for long with the farmer or with any of the men that followed him. Goffredo had a narrow escape,' Cesare opined, lean, strong face grim, well aware that his laid-back and rather naive father could never have coped with so fickle a wife.

'So, why has your father sent you that file?'

'He's trying to get me interested in the on-going, "Lionos reclamation project",' Cesare said very drily, the slant of his wide, sensual mouth expressing sardonic amusement as he sketched mocking quotations marks in the air.

'He actually thinks he has a chance of per-suading *you* to consider marriage with one of those two women?' Jonathan slowly shook his head for neither female appeared to be a show-stopper and Cesare enjoyed the repu-tation of being a connoisseur of the female sex. 'Is he crazy?'

'Always an optimist.' Cesare sighed. 'In the same way he never listens when I tell him I haven't the smallest desire to ever get married.'

'As a happily married man and father, I have to tell you that you're missing out.'

Cesare resisted a rude urge to roll his eyes in mockery. He knew that, in spite of the odds, good marriages *did* exist. His fa-ther had one, after all, and evidently Jona-than did too. But Cesare had no faith in true love and happy-ever-after stories, particularly not when his own first love had ditched him to waltz down the aisle with an extremely wealthy man, who referred to himself as being seventy-five years young. Serafina had dutifully proclaimed her love of older men all the way to the graveyard gates and was now a very rich widow, who had been chasing Cesare in the hope of a rematch ever since.

Cesare's recollections were tinged with supreme scorn. He would never make a mistake like Serafina again. It had been a boy's mistake, he reminded himself wryly. He was now far less ignorant about the nature of the female sex. He had never yet lavished his wealth on a woman who wasn't more excited by his money than by anything else he offered. A satisfied smile softened the hard line of his wide, expressive mouth when he thought of his current lover, a gorgeous French fashion model who went to great lengths to please him in bed and out of it. And all without the fatal suffocating commitment of rings or nagging or noisy kids attached. What was not to like? It was true that he was an extremely generous lover but what was money for but enjoyment when you had as much as Cesare now had?

Cesare was less amused and indeed he tensed when he strolled into his city penthouse that evening to receive the news from his manservant, Primo, that his father had arrived for an unexpected visit.

Goffredo was out on the roof terrace admiring the panoramic view of London when Cesare joined him.

'To what do I owe the honour?' he mocked.

His father, always an extrovert in the affection stakes, clasped his son in a hug as if he hadn't seen the younger man in months rather than mere weeks. 'I need to talk to you about your grandmother...'

Cesare's smile immediately faded. 'What's wrong?'

Goffredo grimaced. 'Athene needs a coronary bypass. Hopefully it will relieve her angina.'

Cesare had stilled, a frown line etched between his level ebony brows. 'She's seventy-five.'

'The prognosis for her recovery is excellent,' his father told him reassuringly. 'Unfortunately the real problem is my mother's outlook on life. She thinks she's too old for surgery. She thinks she's had her three score years and ten and should be grateful for it.'

'That's ridiculous. If necessary, I'll go and talk some sense into her,' Cesare said impatiently.

'She needs something to look forward to… some motivation to make her believe that the pain and stress of surgery will be worthwhile.'

Cesare released his breath in a slow hiss. 'I hope you're not talking about Lionos. That's nothing but a pipe dream.'

Goffredo studied his only son with compressed lips. 'Since when have you been defeatist about any challenge?'

'I'm too clever to tilt at windmills,' Cesare said drily.

'But surely you have some imagination? Some…what is it you chaps call it now? The ability to think outside the box?' the older man persisted. 'Times have changed, Cesare. The world has moved on and when it comes to the island you have a power that I was never blessed with.'

Cesare heaved a sigh and wished he had worked late at the office where pure calm and self-discipline ruled, the very building blocks of his lifestyle. 'And what power would that be?' he asked reluctantly.

'You are incredibly wealthy and the current owners of the island are dirt-poor.'

'But the will is watertight.'

'Money could be a great persuader,' his

father reasoned. 'You don't want a wife and probably neither of Francesca's daughters wants a real husband at such a young age. Why can't you come to some sort of business arrangement with one of them?'

Cesare shook his arrogant dark head. 'You're asking me to try and get round the will?'

'The will has already been minutely appraised by a top inheritance lawyer in Rome. If you can marry one of those girls, you will have the right to visit the island and, what is more important, you will have the right to take your grandmother there,' Goffredo outlined, clearly expecting his son to be impressed by that revelation.

Instead, Cesare suppressed a groan of impatience. 'And what's that worth at the end of the day? It's *not* ownership, it's *not* getting the island back into the family.'

'Even a visit after all the years that have passed would be a source of great joy to your grandmother,' Goffredo pointed out in a tone of reproach.

'I always understood that visiting the island was against the terms of the will.'

'Not if a marriage has first taken place. That is a distinction that it took a lawyer to point out. Certainly, if any of us were to visit without that security, Francesca's daughters would forfeit their inheritance and the island would go to the government by default.'

'Which would please no one but the government,' Cesare conceded wryly. 'Do you really think that a measly visit to the island would mean that much to Nonna?' he pressed.

'The right to pay her respects again at her parents' graves? To see the house where she was born and where she married and first lived with my father? She has many happy memories of Lionos.'

'But would one short visit satisfy her? It's my belief that she has always dreamt of living out her life there and that's out of the question because a child has to be born to fulfil the full terms of the will and grant us the right to put down roots on the island again.'

'There is a very good chance that clause could be set aside in court as unreasonable. Human rights law has already altered many matters once set in stone,' Goffredo reasoned with enthusiasm.

'It's doubtful,' Cesare argued. 'It would take many years and a great deal of money to take it to court and the government would naturally fight any change we sought. The court option won't work in my lifetime. And what woman is going to marry and have a child with me, to allow me to inherit an un-inhabited, undeveloped island? Even if I did offer to buy the island from her once we were married.'

It was his father's turn to groan. 'You must know how much of a catch you are, Cesare. *Madre di Dio*, you've been beating the women off with a stick since you were a teenager!'

Cesare dealt him an amused look. 'And you don't think it would be a little immoral to conceive a child for such a purpose?'

'As I've already stated,' Goffredo pro-claimed with dignity, 'I am not suggesting you go *that* far.'

'But I couldn't reclaim the island for the family *without* going that far,' Cesare fielded very drily. 'And if I can't buy it or gain any-thing beyond guaranteeing Nonna the right to visit the wretched place one more time, what is the point of approaching some stranger and trying to bribe her?'

'Is that your last word on the subject?' his father asked stiffly when the silence dragged.

'I'm a practical man,' Cesare murmured wryly. 'If we could regain the island I could see some point of pursuing this.'

The older man halted on his passage towards the door and turned back to face his son with compressed lips. 'You could at least approach Francesca's daughters and see if something could be worked out. You could at least *try...*'

When his father departed in high dudgeon, Cesare swore long and low in frustration. Goffredo was so temperamental and so easily carried away. He was good at getting bright ideas but not so smooth with the follow-up or the fallout. His son, on the other hand, never let emotion or sentiment cloud his judgement and rarely got excited about anything.

Even so, Cesare did break into a sweat when he thought about his grandmother's need for surgery and her lack of interest in having it. In his opinion, Athene was probably bored and convinced that life had no further interesting challenges to offer. She was also probably a little frightened of the surgical procedure as well. His grandmother was such a strong and courageous woman that people frequently failed to recognise that she had her fears and weaknesses just like everyone else.

Cesare's own mother had died on the day he was born and Goffredo's Greek mother,

Athene, had come to her widowed son's rescue. While Goffredo had grieved and struggled to build up his first business and establish some security, Athene had taken charge of raising Cesare. Even before he'd started school he had been playing chess, reading and doing advanced maths for enjoyment. His grandmother had been quick to recognise her grandson's prodigious intellectual gifts. Unlike his father, she had not been intimidated by his genius IQ and against a background of loving support Athene had given Cesare every opportunity to flourish and develop at his own pace. He owed his *nonna* a great deal and she was still the only woman in the world whom Cesare had ever truly cared about. But then he had never been an emotional man, had never been able to understand or feel truly comfortable around more demonstrative personalities. He was astute, level-headed and controlled in every field of his life yet he had a soft spot in his heart for his grandmother that he would not have admitted to a living soul.

A business arrangement, Cesare ruminated broodingly, flicking open the file again. There was no prospect of him approaching the teenager but the plain young woman in the woolly hat and old coat? Could he even contemplate such a gross and unsavoury lowering of his high standards? He was conservative in his tastes and not an easy man to please but if the prize was great enough, he was clever enough to compromise and adapt, wasn't he? Aware that very few people were cleverer than he was, Cesare contemplated the startling idea of getting married and grimaced with distaste at the threat of being forced to live in such close contact with another human being.

'You should've sent Hero off to the knackers when I told you to!' Brian Whitaker bit out in disgust. 'Instead you've kept him eating his head off in that stable. How can we afford that with the cost of feed what it is?'

'Chrissie's very fond of Hero. She's coming home from uni next week and I wanted her to have the chance to say goodbye.' Lizzie kept her voice low rather than risk stoking her father's already irascible temper. The older man was standing by the kitchen table, his trembling hands—the most visible symptom of the Parkinson's disease that had ravaged his once strong body—braced on the chair back as he glowered at his daughter, his gaunt, weathered face grim with censure.

'And if you do that, she'll weep and she'll wail and she'll try to talk you out of it again. What's the point of that? You tried to sell him and there were no takers,' he reminded her with biting impatience. 'You're a bloody *useless* farmer, Lizzie!'

'That horse charity across the valley may have a space coming up this week,' Lizzie told him, barely even flinching from her father's scorn because his dissatisfaction was so familiar to her. 'I was hoping for the best.'

'Since when has hoping for the best paid the bills?' Brian demanded with withering contempt. 'Chrissie should be home here helping you, not wasting her time studying!'

Lizzie compressed her lips, wincing at the idea that her kid sister should also sacrifice her education to their daily struggle for survival against an ever-increasing tide of debt. The farm was failing but it had been failing for a long time. Unfortunately her father had never approved of Chrissie's desire to go to university. His world stopped at the borders of the farm and he had very little interest in anything beyond it. Lizzie understood his reasoning because her world had shrunk to the same boundaries once she had left school at sixteen.

At the same time, though, she adored the kid sister she had struggled to protect throughout their dysfunctional childhood and was willing to take a lot of grief from her father if it meant that the younger woman could enjoy the youthful freedom and opportunities that she herself had been denied. In fact Lizzie had been as proud as any mother when Chrissie had won a place to study Literature at Oxford. Although she missed Chrissie, she would not have wished her own life of back-breaking toil and isolation on anyone she loved.

As Lizzie dug her feet back into her muddy boots a small low-slung shaggy dog, whose oddly proportioned body reflected his very mixed ancestry, greeted her at the back door with his feeding bowl in his mouth.

'Oh, I'm so sorry, Archie…I forgot about you,' Lizzie groaned, climbing out of the boots again to trudge back across the kitchen floor and fill the dog bowl. While she mentally listed all the many, many tasks she had yet to accomplish she heard the reassuring roar of a football game playing on the television in the room next door and some of the tension eased from her slight shoulders. Watching some sport and forgetting his aches and pains for a little while would put her father in a better mood.

Her father was a difficult man, but then his life had always been challenging. In his case hard work and commitment to the farm had failed to pay off. He had taken on the farm tenancy at a young age and had always had to work alone. Her late mother, Francesca, had only lasted a few years as a farmer's wife before running off with a man she deemed to have more favourable prospects. Soured by the divorce that followed, Brian Whitaker had not remarried. When Lizzie was twelve, Francesca had died suddenly and her father had been landed with the responsibility of two daughters who were practically strangers to him. The older man had done his best even though he could never resist an opportunity to remind Lizzie that she would never be the strong capable son he had wanted and needed to help him on the farm. He had barely passed fifty when ill health had handicapped him and prevented him from doing physical work.

Lizzie knew she was a disappointment to the older man but then she was used to falling short of other people's expectations.

Her mother had longed for a more outgoing, fun-loving child than shy, socially awkward Lizzie had proved to be. Her father had wanted a son, not a daughter. Even her fiancé had left her for a woman who seemed to be a far more successful farmer's wife than Lizzie could ever have hoped to be. Sadly, Lizzie had become accustomed to not measuring up and had learned to simply get on with the job at hand rather than dwell on her own deficiencies.

She started her day off with the easy task of feeding the hens and gathering the eggs. Then she fed Hero, whose feed she was buying solely from her earnings from working Saturday nights behind the bar of the village pub. She didn't earn a wage at home for her labour. How could she take a wage out of the kitty every week when the rising overdraft at the bank was a constant worry? Household bills, feed and fuel costs were necessities that had to come out of that overdraft and she was dreading the arrival of yet another warning letter from the bank.

She loaded the slurry tank to spray the meadow field before her father could complain about how far behind she was with the spring schedule. Archie leapt into the tractor cab with her and sat panting by her side. He still wore the old leather collar punched with his name that he had arrived with. When she had found him wandering the fields, hungry and bedraggled, Lizzie had reckoned he had been dumped at the side of the road and, sadly, nobody had ever come looking for him. She suspected that his formerly expensive collar revealed that he had once been a much-loved pet, possibly abandoned because his elderly owner had passed away.

When he'd first arrived, he had hung out with their aging sheepdog, Shep, and had demonstrated a surprising talent for picking up Shep's skills so that when Shep had died even Brian Whitaker had acknowledged that Archie could make himself useful round the farm. Lizzie, on the other hand, utterly adored Archie. He curled up at her feet in bed at night and allowed himself to be cuddled whenever she was low.

She was driving back to the yard to refill the slurry tank when she saw a long, sleek, glossy black car filtering off the main road into the farm lane. Her brow furrowed at the sight. She couldn't picture anyone coming in a car that big and expensive to buy the free-range eggs she sold. Parking the tractor by the fence, she climbed out with Archie below one arm, stooping to let her pet down.

That was Cesare's first glimpse of Lizzie. She glanced up as she unbent and the limo slowed to ease past the tractor. He saw that though she might dress like a bag lady she had skin as translucent as the finest porcelain and eyes the colour of prized jade. He breathed in deep and slow.

His driver got out of the car only to come under immediate attack by what was clearly a vicious dog but which more closely resembled a scruffy fur muff on short legs. As the woman captured the dog to restrain it and before his driver could open the door for him Cesare sprang out and instantly the offensive stench of the farm yard assaulted his fastidious nostrils. His intense concentration trained on his quarry, he simply held his breath while lazily wondering if she smelt as well. When his father had said the Whitaker family was dirt-poor he had clearly not been joking. The farmhouse bore no resemblance to a picturesque country cottage with roses round the door. The rain guttering sagged, the windows needed replacing and the paint was peeling off the front door.

'Are you looking for directions?' Lizzie

asked as the tall black-haired male emerged in a fluid shift of long limbs from the rear seat.

Cesare straightened and straight away focused on her pouty pink mouth. That was three unexpected pluses in a row, he acknowledged in surprise. Lizzie Whitaker had great skin, beautiful eyes and a mouth that made a man think of sinning, and Cesare had few inhibitions when it came to the sins of sexual pleasure. Indeed, his hot-blooded nature and need for regular sex were the two traits he deemed potential weaknesses, he acknowledged wryly.

'Directions?' he queried, disconcerted by the disruptive drift of his own thoughts, anathema to his self-discipline. In spite of his exasperation, his mind continued to pick up on the fact that Lizzie Whitaker was small, possibly only a few inches over five feet tall, and seemingly slender below the wholly dreadful worn and stained green jacket and baggy workman's overalls she wore beneath. The woolly hat pulled low on her brow made her eyes look enormous as she stared up at him much as if he'd stepped out of a spaceship in front of her.

One glance at the stranger had reduced Lizzie to gaping in an almost spellbound moment out of time. He was simply…*stunning* from his luxuriant black hair to his dark-as-bitter-chocolate deep-set eyes and strong, uncompromisingly masculine jawline. In truth she had never ever seen a more dazzling man and that disconcertingly intimate thought froze her in place like a tongue-tied schoolgirl.

'I assumed you were lost,' Lizzie explained weakly, finding it a challenge to fill her lungs with oxygen while he looked directly at her with eyes that, even lit by the weak spring sunshine, shifted to a glorious shade of bronzed gold. For a split second, she felt as if she were drowning and she shook her head slightly, struggling to think straight and act normally, her colour rising steadily as she fought the unfamiliar lassitude engulfing her.

'No, I'm not lost… This *is* the Whitaker farm?'

'Yes, I'm Lizzie Whitaker…'

Only the British could take a pretty name like Elisabetta and shorten it to something so commonplace, Cesare decided irritably. 'I'm Cesare Sabatino.'

Her jade eyes widened. His foreign-sounding name was meaningless to her ears because she barely recognised a syllable of it. 'Sorry, I didn't catch that…'

His beautifully sensual mouth quirked. 'You don't speak Italian?'

'The odd word, not much. Are you Italian?' Lizzie asked, feeling awkward as soon as she realised that he somehow knew that her mother had been of Italian extraction. Francesca had actually planned to raise her daughters to be bilingual but Brian Whitaker had objected vehemently to the practice as soon as his children began using words he couldn't understand and from that point on English had become the only language in their home.

'*Sì*, I'm Italian,' Cesare confirmed, sliding a lean brown hand into his jacket to withdraw a business card and present it to her. The extraordinary grace of his every physical gesture also ensnared her attention and she had to force her gaze down to the card.

Unfortunately, his name was no more comprehensible to Lizzie when she saw it printed. 'Your name's Caesar,' she pronounced with some satisfaction.

A muscle tugged at the corner of his unsmiling mouth. 'Not Caesar. We're not in ancient Rome. It's Chay-zar-ray,' he sounded out with perfect diction, his exotic accent underlining every syllable with a honeyed mellifluence that spiralled sinuously round her to create the strangest sense of dislocation.

'Chay-zar-ray,' she repeated politely while thinking that it was a heck of a fussy mouthful for a first name and that Caesar would have been much more straightforward. 'And you're here *because*...?'

Cesare stiffened, innate aggression powering him at that facetious tone. He was not accustomed to being prompted to get to the point faster and as if the dog had a sensor tracking his mood it began growling soft and low. 'May we go indoors to discuss that?'

Bemused by the effect he was having on her and fiercely irritated by his take-charge manner, Lizzie lifted her chin. 'Couldn't we just talk here? This is the middle of my working day,' she told him truthfully.

Cesare gritted his perfect white teeth and shifted almost imperceptibly closer. The dog loosed a warning snarl and clamped his teeth to the corner of his cashmere overcoat, pulling at it. Cesare sent a winging glance down at the offending animal.

'Archie, *no*!' Lizzie intervened. 'I'm afraid he's very protective of me.'

Archie tugged and tugged at the corner of

the overcoat and failed to shift Cesare an inch further away from his quarry. To the best of his ability Cesare ignored the entire canine assault.

'Oh, for goodness' sake, Archie!' Lizzie finally exclaimed, crouching down to physically detach the dog's jaw from the expensive cloth, noting in dismay that a small tear had been inflicted and cherishing little hope that the damage would not be noted.

Whoever he was, Cesare Sabatino wore clothing that looked incredibly expensive and fitted too well to be anything other than individually designed for its wearer. He wore a faultlessly tailored black suit below the coat and his highly polished shoes were marred only by the skiff of mud that continually covered the yard at damp times of the year. He looked like a high-powered businessman, tycoon or some such thing. Why on earth was such a man coming to visit the farm?

'Are you from our bank?' Lizzie asked abruptly.

'No. I am a businessman,' Cesare admitted calmly.

'You're here to see my father for some reason?' Lizzie prompted apprehensively.

'No…I'm here to see you,' Cesare framed

succinctly as she scrambled upright clutching the still-growling dog to her chest.

'*Me?*' Lizzie exclaimed in astonishment, her gaze colliding with glittering eyes that gleamed like highly polished gold, enhanced by the thick black velvet fringe of his long lashes. Below her clothes, her nipples pinched almost painfully tight and a flare of sudden heat darted down into her pelvis, making her feel extremely uncomfortable. 'Why on earth would you want to see me? Oh, come indoors, if you must,' she completed wearily. 'But I warn you, it's a mess.'

Trudging to the side of the house, Lizzie kicked off her boots and thrust the door open on the untidy kitchen.

Cesare's nostrils flared as he scanned the cluttered room, taking in the pile of dishes heaped in the sink and the remains of some-one's meal still lying on the pine table. Well, he certainly wouldn't be marrying her for her housekeeping skills, he reflected grimly as the dog slunk below the table to continue growling unabated and his reluctant hostess removed her coat and yanked off her woolly hat before hurriedly clearing the table and yanking out a chair for him.

'Coffee…or tea?' Lizzie enquired.

Cesare's entire attention was still locked to the wealth of silver-coloured silky hair that, freed from the woolly hat, now tumbled round her shoulders. It was gorgeous in spite of the odd murky brown tips of colour that damaged the effect. Dip-dying, he thought dimly, vaguely recalling the phrase being used by one of his team who had showed up at the office one day with ludicrously colourful half-blonde, half-pink locks. He blinked, black lashes long as fly swats momentarily concealing his bemused gaze.

'Coffee,' he replied, feeling that he was being very brave and polite in the face of the messy kitchen and standards of hygiene that he suspected might be much lower than he was used to receiving.

In a graceful movement, he doffed his coat and draped it across the back of a chair. Lizzie filled the kettle at the sink and put it on the hotplate on the ancient coal-fired cooking range while taking in the full effect of her visitor's snazzy appearance. He looked like a city slicker who belonged on a glossy magazine cover, the sort of publication that showed how fashion-conscious men should dress. To a woman used to men wearing dirty, often unkempt clothing suitable for outdoor work, he had all the appeal of a fantasy. He really was physically beautiful in every possible way and so unfamiliar was she with that level of male magnetism that she was challenged to drag her eyes from his lean, powerful figure.

Dredging her thoughts from the weird sticking point they had reached, she went to the door of the lounge. A businessman, she reminded herself doggedly. Successful businessmen—and he looked *very* successful— were cold-blooded, calculating individuals, ready to do anything for profit and divorced from sentiment. He certainly emanated that arrogant vibe with his polished image that was so totally inappropriate for a male visiting a working farm. 'Dad? We have a visitor. Do you want tea?'

'A visitor?' Brian Whitaker rose with a frown from his chair and came with shuffling, poorly balanced steps into the kitchen.

Lizzie removed mugs from the cupboard while the two men introduced themselves.

'I'm here about the island that Lizzie and her sister inherited from your late wife,' Cesare explained calmly.

The silence of astonishment engulfed his companions. Lizzie studied him wide-eyed while her father turned his head towards him in a frowning attitude of incredulity.

'It's a rubbish inheritance…nothing but a bad joke!' Lizzie's father contended in a burst of unrestrained bitterness. 'It stands to reason that an inheritance you can't use or sell is worthless… What use is that to anyone? So, that's why you're here? Another fool chasing the pot of gold at the end of the rainbow?'

'Dad!' Lizzie exclaimed in consternation at the older man's blatant scorn.

She wished she had guessed why the Italian had come to visit and scolded herself for not immediately making the association between his nationality and the legacy left to her and Chrissie by their mother. Over the years the island that couldn't be sold had been a source of much bitterness in her family, particularly when money was in such short supply. She lifted the kettle off the range and hastily made the drinks while she wondered what on earth Cesare hoped to achieve by visiting them.

'I'll put your tea in the lounge, Dad,' she said, keen to remove her father from the dialogue, afraid of what he might say in his blunt and challenging way.

Brian Whitaker stole a glance at the Italian's shuttered dark face, not displeased by the effect of having had his say. 'I'll leave you to it, then. After all, the only reason *he* could be here is that he's coming a-courting!' he completed with a derisive laugh that sent a hot tide of colour flaring below Lizzie's pale skin. 'Good luck to you! Lizzie was ditched by the neighbour a couple of years ago and she hasn't been out on a date since then!'

CHAPTER TWO

LIZZIE WANTED THE tiled floor to open up and swallow her where she stood. Being humiliated in front of a stranger felt even more painful than the snide comments and pitying appraisals from the village locals that had followed the ending of her engagement to Andrew Brook two years earlier. A month later, Andrew had married Esther, who had already been pregnant with their son. She stiffened her facial muscles, made the tea and the coffee and even contrived to politely ask if the visitor took sugar.

Wide, sensual mouth set in a grim line, Cesare surveyed Lizzie's rigid back view, noting the narrow cut of her waist and the slender, delicate curves merely hinted at by the overalls. Her father had been cruel taking her down like that in front of an audience. Not a date since, though? He was astonished because, unflattering as her clothing was, Cesare had immediately recognised that she was a beauty. Not perhaps a conventional beauty, he was willing to admit, not the kind of beauty that set the world on fire but certainly the type that should make the average male look more than once. What was wrong with the local men?

'Sorry about Dad,' Lizzie apologised in a brittle voice, setting the coffee down carefully on the table in front of him, catching the evocative scent of some citrusy cologne as she briefly leant closer and stiffening as a result of the sudden warmth pooling in her pelvis. Never had anyone made her feel more uncomfortable in her own home.

'You don't need to apologise, *cara*,' Cesare parried.

'But I should explain. My parents resented the will—personally, I never think about it. Unfortunately, the island was a sore point in our lives when I was a child because money was tight.'

'Have you ever visited Lionos?'

'No, I've never had the opportunity. Mum went once with one of her boyfriends and stayed for a week. She wasn't too impressed,' Lizzie revealed ruefully while she scanned his lean, strong face, taking in the high cheek-bones, straight nose and hard, masculine mouth before involuntarily sliding her gaze upward again to take another sweep of those absolutely devastating dark golden eyes of his. 'I think Mum was expecting luxury but I believe the accommodation was more basic.'

'The will endowed the island with a trust and I understand a caretaker and his family live nearby to maintain the property.'

Lizzie cocked her head to one side, her shattered nerves slowly stabilising at his lack of comment about her father's outburst. Pale, silky hair slid across her cheekbone and Cesare looked up into those wide hazel-green eyes framed with soft honey-brown lashes, and suddenly he was aware of the heavy pulse of heat at his groin and the muscles in his broad shoulders pulled taut as ropes as he resisted that sirens' call of lust with all his might.

'Yes. But the trust only covers maintenance costs, not improvements, and I understand that the house is still firmly stuck in the thirties. Mum also assumed that the caretaker would cook and clean for them but instead the man and his wife told her that they weren't servants and she had to look after herself,'

Lizzie volunteered wryly. 'All in all she found it a very expensive jaunt by the time they'd paid someone to take them out to the island and deliver food while they were there.'

'Naturally you want to know what I'm doing here,' Cesare murmured smoothly.

'Well, I don't think you've come a-courting,' Lizzie fielded with a shrug that dismissed her father's gibe but completely failed to hide her discomfiture at that crack.

'Not in the conventional sense,' Cesare agreed, lean fingers flexing round the mug of coffee. It was barely drinkable but he doubted if she expended much concern when it came to the domestic front, which was hardly surprising when it was obvious that she was struggling to keep the farm afloat single-handedly. She was leaning back against the cooking range with defensively folded arms, trying to appear relaxed but visibly as tense as a bow string. 'But I do think we might be able to come to a business arrangement.'

Lizzie frowned, dragging her wandering gaze from his lean, extravagantly handsome features with a slight rise of colour, scolding herself for her lack of concentration, questioning what it was about him that kept her looking back at him again and again, long after curiosity should have been satisfied. 'A business arrangement?'

'I don't think your sister enters this as she's still a teenager. Obviously as co-owner of the island, you would have to confer with her, but I'm willing to offer you a substantial amount of money to go through a marriage ceremony with me.'

Her lashes fluttered in shock because he had knocked her for six. Inexplicably, his cool sophistication and smooth delivery made the fantastic proposition he had just made seem almost workaday and acceptable. 'Seriously? *Just* a marriage ceremony? But what would you get out of that?'

Cesare told her about his grandmother's deep attachment to the island and her approaching surgery. As she listened, Lizzie nodded slowly, strangely touched by the softer tone he couldn't help employing when talking about the old lady. His screened gaze and the faint hint of flush along his spectacular cheekbones encouraged her scrutiny to linger with helpless curiosity. He was not quite as cold and tough as he seemed on the surface, she acknowledged in surprise. But she could see that he was very uncomfortable with showing emotion.

'Isn't circumventing the will against the law?' she prompted in a small voice.

'I wasn't planning to publicise the fact. For the sake of appearances we would have to pretend that the marriage was the real deal for a few months at least.'

'And the "having a child" bit? Where does that come in?' Lizzie could not resist asking.

'Whether it comes into our arrangement or not is up to you. I will pay generously for the right to take my grandmother to the island for a visit and if we were to contrive to meet the *full* terms of the will, you and your sister would stand to collect a couple of million pounds, at the very least, from selling Lionos to me,' he spelt out quietly. 'I am an extremely wealthy man and I will pay a high price to bring the island back into my family.'

Millions? Lizzie's mouth ran dry and she lost colour, eyes dropping to focus on the long, lean brown fingers gracefully coiled round the mug of coffee. For a split second she saw her every hope and dream fulfilled by ill-gotten gains. Her father could give up the farm tenancy, and she and Chrissie could buy him a house in the village where he would be able to go to the pub quizzes he loved and meet up with his cronies. Chrissie would be able to chuck in her two part-time jobs, concentrate on her studies and pay off her student loans. Being freed from the burden of the farm would enable Lizzie to go and train for a job she would enjoy. Archie could get some professional grooming and a new collar and live on the very best pet food...

It became an increasingly stupid dream and she reddened with mortification, hands clenching by her side as she suppressed her wild imaginings in shame at how susceptible she had been when tempted by the equivalent of a lottery win.

'I couldn't have a child with a stranger... or bring a child into the world for such a purpose,' she confided. 'But if it's any consolation, just for a minute there I wished I was the sort of woman who could.'

'Think it over,' Cesare suggested, having registered without surprise that the suggestion of oodles of cash had finally fully engaged her in their discussion. He rose fluidly upright and tapped the business card he had left on the table top. 'My cell number.'

He was very big, possibly a foot taller than she was, with broad shoulders, narrow hips and long, powerful legs.

'Yes, well, there's a lot to think over,' she muttered uneasily.

He reached for his coat and turned back to her, dark eyes bright and shimmering as topaz in sunshine. 'There are two options and either will bring in a profit for you.'

'You definitely talk like a businessman,' she remarked, unimpressed by the statement, ashamed of her temporary dive into a fantasy land where every sheep had a proverbial golden fleece. Could it really be that easy to go from being a decent person to a mercenary one? she was asking herself worriedly.

'I am trying to negotiate a business arrangement,' he pointed out drily.

'Was it *your* father who once asked my mother to marry him?' Lizzie could not stop herself from enquiring. 'Or was that someone from another branch of your family?'

Cesare came to a halt. 'No, that was my father and it wasn't a business proposal. He fell hard for your mother and they were engaged when she came over here on holiday. Having met your father, however, she preferred him,' he advanced without any expression at all.

But Lizzie recognised the unspoken disapproval in the hard bones of his lean, strong face and she flushed because her mother had been decidedly changeable in her affections and there was no denying the fact. Predictably, Francesca had never admitted that she had actually got engaged to their father's predecessor. But then every man that came along had been the love of Francesca's life until either he revealed his true character or someone else seized her interest. Her mother had always moved on without a backward glance, never once pausing to try and work on a relationship or considering the cost of such continual upheaval in the lives of her two young children.

'I'm afraid I'm not a sentimental man,' Cesare imparted. 'I'm innately practical in every way. Why shouldn't you make what you can of your inheritance for your family's benefit?'

'Because it just doesn't seem right,' Lizzie confided uncertainly. 'It's not what my great-grandfather intended either when he drew up that will.'

'No, he wanted revenge because my grandmother's brother jilted his daughter at the altar. My great-uncle was in the wrong but plunging the island into legal limbo simply to keep it out of my family's hands was no more justifiable,' Cesare countered with complete assurance. 'It's been that way for nearly eighty years but I believe that we have the power to change that.'

'The ethics involved aren't something I've ever thought about,' Lizzie admitted, resisting the urge to confess that the island still seemed no more real to her than that fabled pot of gold at the end of the rainbow that her father had mentioned.

Cesare smiled with sudden brilliance, amused by her honesty and her lack of pretence.

His smile almost blinded her, illuminating his lean, darkly handsome face, and she wanted so badly to touch him for a disconcerting moment that she clenched her hands into fists to restrain herself. She was deeply disturbed by the effect he had on her. Indeed, she feared it because she recognised her reaction for the fierce physical attraction that it was. And nobody knew better than Francesca Whitaker's daughter how dangerous giving rein to such mindless responses could be for it had propelled her mother into one disastrous relationship after another.

In the smouldering silence, beautiful, dark golden eyes fringed with velvet black held hers and she trembled, fighting reactions she had never experienced so powerfully before.

'My offer's on the table and I'm willing to negotiate with you. Discuss it with your sister and your father but urge them to keep the matter confidential,' Cesare advised smoothly, staring down into her upturned face, attention lingering on the lush contours of her lips as he wondered what she would *taste* like. 'We could go the full distance on this... I find you appealing.'

And with that deeply unsettling comment, Cesare Sabatino swung on his heel and strode back out to the limousine sitting ready to depart. The driver leapt out to throw open the door for his passenger and Cesare lowered his proud dark head and climbed in.

Appealing? Lizzie pushed her hair back off her brow and caught her surprised reflection in the small age-spotted mirror on the wall. He was really saying that he could go to bed with her and conceive a child with her if she was willing: that was what he meant by the word *appealing*. Her face flamed. She was *not* willing. She also knew the difference between right and wrong. She knew that more money didn't necessarily mean more happiness and that a child was usually better off with a mother *and* a father.

Yet the image of the tiny boy she had

glimpsed cradled in her former fiancé's arms after the child's christening in the church had pierced Lizzie with a pain greater than that inflicted by Andrew's infidelity. Lizzie had always wanted a baby and ached at the sight of infants. When Andrew had left her for Esther, she had envied Esther for her son, *not* her husband. What did that say about her? That she was as cold at heart and frigid as Andrew had once accused her of being? Even remembering that hurtful indictment, Lizzie winced and felt less than other women, knowing that she had been tried and found wanting by a young man who had only wanted a warm and loving wife. Lizzie knew that, in choosing Esther, Andrew had made the right decision for them both. Yet Lizzie had loved Andrew too in her way.

Her eyes stung with moisture, her fingers toying with the ends of the brown-tinted hair that Andrew had persuaded her to dye. The dye was growing out, a reminder of how foolish a woman could be when she tried to change herself to please a man...

But where on earth had her strong maternal instinct come from? Certainly not from her volatile mother, who in the grip of her wild infatuations had always focused her energies on the man in her life. Lizzie had not been surprised to learn of the impetuous way Francesca had evidently ditched Cesare's father to marry Lizzie's father instead. Hard Yorkshire winters and life on a shoestring, however, had dimmed Brian Whitaker's appeal for her mother and within weeks of Chrissie's birth Francesca had run off with a man who had turned out to be a drunk. His successor had been more interested in spending Francesca's recent legacy following the death of her Italian parents than in Francesca herself. Her third lover had been repeatedly unfaithful. And the fourth, who married her, had been violent.

Lizzie had always found it very hard to trust men after living through her mother's grim roll call of destructive relationships. She had struggled to protect the sister five years her junior from the constant fallout of moving home and changing schools, striving to ensure that her sibling could still enjoy her childhood and wasn't forced to grow up as quickly as Lizzie had. Almost all the happy moments in Lizzie's life had occurred when Chrissie was young and Lizzie had the comfort of knowing that her love and care was both wanted and needed by her sibling. When her sister left home to go to university it had opened a vast hole in Lizzie's life. Archie had partially filled that hole, a reality that made her grin and shrug off her deep and troubled thoughts with the acknowledgement that it was time to get back to work and concentrate on what really mattered.

'Marry him and stop making such a production out of it!' Brian Whitaker snapped at his daughter angrily. 'We don't have any other choice. The rent is going up and the bank's on the brink of calling in our loan!'

'It's not that simple, Dad,' Lizzie began to argue again.

But the older man wasn't listening. He hadn't listened to a word his daughter had said since the letter from the bank had delivered its lethal warning. 'Simple would have been you marrying Andrew. He would have taken on the tenancy. I could still have lived here. Everyone would have been happy but could you pull it off?' he derided. '*No*, you had to play fast and loose with him, wanting to *wait* to get married!'

'I wanted to get to know him properly, not rush in. I wanted our marriage to last,' Lizzie protested.

'You might as well have parcelled him up for Esther and handed him over. Andrew was our one chance to keep this place afloat and you threw him away,' he condemned bitterly. 'Now you're mouthing off about all the reasons why you can't marry a man and have a child just to improve *all* our lives!'

'A lot of women wouldn't want to do it!' It was Lizzie's parting shot, tossed over her shoulder as she stomped back into the yard with Archie dancing at her heels. A week had passed since Cesare Sabatino's visit and her father had reasoned and condemned and outright ranted at her every day for her reluctance to accept Cesare's proposal.

Hopefully, Chrissie would not be singing the same tune, Lizzie reflected ruefully as she drove her father's ancient, battered Land Rover Defender down the lane to collect her sister off the train. She had told Chrissie all about Cesare's visit on the phone and her sibling had urged her to follow her conscience and refuse to pay heed to her father's grievances.

That was, however, proving a much more major challenge than she had expected, Lizzie acknowledged heavily. Almost insurmountable problems were forming ahead of her like a string of dangerous obstacles. They could not afford to pay a higher rent when the tenancy came up for renewal and that reality would render them homeless. They could not even afford to live if the bank demanded that the loan be repaid as they were threatening to do. And *where* would they live, if the worst came to the worst? Her father had no savings. Yes, it was all very well following her conscience, Lizzie conceded wretchedly, but right now it was no good at all as a blueprint for economic survival.

Sadly, the stress of the constant arguments and anxiety was taking the edge off Lizzie's usual happy anticipation at the prospect of having her sister home for a couple of days. Chrissie, pale silver hair caught up in a sensible ponytail, blue eyes sparkling with affection, was waiting outside the station, two big cases by her side and a bulging rucksack on her slender shoulders.

'My goodness, you've brought back a lot of luggage…but it's not the end of term,' Lizzie remarked in bewilderment, thinking out loud while Chrissie concentrated on giving her a fierce hug of welcome.

'I've missed you so much,' her sibling confessed. 'And I'm going to ask you all over again—why have you still not had your hair dyed back to normal?'

'I haven't had the time…or the cash,' Lizzie muttered, hoisting a heavy case and propelling it across to the Land Rover.

'No, you're still punishing yourself for not marrying Andrew.'

'They're teaching you psychology now on your English course?' Lizzie teased.

Luggage stowed, Lizzie drove back home. 'I should warn you…Dad's on the warpath.'

'He wants you to marry the Italian and make our fortunes, right?' Chrissie groaned in despair. 'Dear old Dad, what a dinosaur he is. He tried to pressure you into marrying Andrew for the sake of the farm and now he's trying to serve you up on the altar of that stupid island! Well, you don't need to worry, you're not going to come under any pressure from me on that score. We've lived all our lives without the excitement of being rich and what you don't have, you don't miss!'

In spite of her stress level, Lizzie managed to smile. After an unrelieved overdose of her father's reproaches, Chrissie, with her positive outlook, was like a little ray of sunshine. 'You're right,' she agreed even though she knew that her kid sister was not very grounded. Chrissie had always been a dreamer, the creative one with the fluffy romantic and idealistic ideas.

In fact, while she watched Chrissie hurtle across the yard to pet her elderly pony, Hero, and feed him an apple from her pocket, her heart sank from so bald a reminder of her sister's tendency to always look on the bright side even if there wasn't one. Didn't Chrissie appreciate that if they lost their home, Hero would be one of the first sacrifices?

'I've got a surprise for you...' Chrissie told her, almost skipping back to Lizzie's side to help her unload her luggage. 'I'm home for good!'

Lizzie turned incredulous eyes on the younger woman. 'What are you talking about?'

'I'm dropping out of uni...I'm coming home,' Chrissie proffered, her soft mouth set in an unusually firm and purposeful line. 'Even with the two jobs and the student loan, I can hardly afford to eat and my overdraft is *massive*, Lizzie. I'm fed up with it, especially when I know you're slogging away here every hour God gives and still barely scratching a living. I'm going to get a job and help you whenever I can. I'm all grown up now—it's past time I pulled my weight on the home front.'

Shock was reverberating through Lizzie, closely followed by dismay. Much as she missed her sister, the very last thing she wanted was to see Chrissie throw away her education to come home and vegetate. In any case, it was a moot point that they would even have a home to offer her sibling in a few weeks' time. 'I didn't realise that you were having such a struggle.'

'I didn't want you worrying,' Chrissie confided. 'But I've learned a lot. I'd no idea it cost so much just to live. I can't possibly work any more hours, though. I've already had a warning from my tutor about my standard of work slipping... I'm so tired I'm falling asleep in lectures.'

And that was the moment when Lizzie reached her decision. What security her family had was vanishing fast but it was within her power to change everything for the better. How could she stand by and simply do nothing for her family while their lives fell apart? At the very least she should go through with the wedding to enable Cesare to take his grandmother back to the island for a visit. Whatever he paid her for that service would surely settle their outstanding bills and enable her to find a rental property in the village. But how could she go further than that? How could she have a child with him so that he could legally buy Lionos and resolve all her family's financial problems?

The answer came to Lizzie in a blinding flash of light and she could barely credit that she had not seen the solution sooner. Cesare had said he was very practical and the answer she came up with would not only make the threat of intimacy with a stranger unnecessary but would also be a supremely sensible approach. Suddenly the sensation of weighty responsibility and dread on her shoulders and spine evaporated and she straightened, even cracking a brief smile at the heady prospect of finally being in full control of her life again.

'You're going back to university on Sunday, young lady,' Lizzie told her kid sister firmly. 'You will quit your part-time jobs and concentrate on your studies. I will ensure that you manage.'

'You can't marry the guy, Lizzie!' Chrissie gasped in horror. 'You simply *can't*!'

Lizzie thought fast and breathed in deep before she sat down at the kitchen table. 'Let me be honest with you. I've spent eight years working round the clock on this farm. I've had no time for friends and I've had very little social life. I have no decent clothes or jewellery and I don't even know how to put on make-up properly.'

'But that doesn't mean you have to give way to Dad and make a sacrifice of yourself.'

'Has it occurred to you that maybe I *want* to marry Cesare and have a child? He's a very handsome man and you know how much I've always wanted a baby. I also would like to have enough money not to worry myself sick every time a bill comes through the letter box!' Lizzie declared, her heart-shaped face taut with vehement composure as she watched Chrissie frown and suddenly look unsure of her ground.

'I'm deadly serious,' Lizzie continued with dogged determination. 'I *want* to marry Cesare. It's the best thing for all of us and, believe me, I'm not the sacrificial type.'

'I never thought…I never dreamt…' Bemused and uncertain of such an explanation from the big sister she had always loved and admired, Chrissie shook her head, frowning at her sibling. 'Are you sure, Lizzie? Have you really thought this through?'

No, Lizzie hadn't thought it all through and

was determined not to run the risk of doing so before she had tied the official knot. Whatever happened she was going to marry Cesare Sabatino and miraculously sort out her own and her father's *and* Chrissie's problems. No other action now made sense. So, it would be scary and would entail deception—well, she would get braver and she would learn some new skills. My goodness, hadn't she just told a barefaced lie to the sister she loved?

She walked into her bedroom and lifted the business card Cesare had left behind. Before she could take fright, she tapped out the number on her mobile phone and then studied the blank message space.

Will agree to marry you. Talk about the rest when we next meet.

Cesare blinked down at the text and then glanced across the dinner table at Celine, whose sleek blonde perfection had entranced him for longer than most women managed. In his mind's eye, however, he was no longer seeing the French fashion model, he was seeing a slender platinum blonde with luminous green eyes surrounded by soft brown lashes. Surprise was cutting through his satisfaction, perhaps because he had had the weirdest conviction that Lizzie Whitaker would say no to the temptation of the cash he had offered. He wondered why he had thought that, why he had assumed she would be different from any other woman.

Women liked money and he liked women: it was a fair exchange in which neither of them need feel used or abused. Hadn't he learned that a long time ago? Athene would be able to return to her childhood home for a visit at the very least. Was Lizzie Whitaker planning to meet the *full* terms of the will? Raw anticipation of an entirely different kind infiltrated Cesare and he frowned, bewildered by the flood of undisciplined hormones smashing his self-control to pieces. He was thinking about Lizzie Whitaker, *only* thinking about her and he was as aroused as a teenager contemplating sex for the first time.

'You seem distracted,' Celine remarked tentatively.

Cesare studied her without an iota of his usual lust, exasperated by the games his body was playing with his usually very well-disciplined brain. 'A business deal,' he proffered truthfully.

Goffredo would be overjoyed at the news

of the upcoming wedding while Cesare was simply stunned at the prospect of getting married, whether it was a business arrangement or not. *Married!* The delicious food on his plate ebbed in appeal. Dense black lashes screened his gaze. It was rare for him to take a night off and somehow Lizzie Whitaker had contrived to kill any notion he had had of relaxing with Celine. What was it about her that unsettled him? After all she was a pretty standard gold-digger, willing to do virtually anything to enrich herself, and how could he criticise her for that reality when he had baited the hook?

CHAPTER THREE

'I DON'T KNOW what the arrangements are likely to be,' Lizzie told her father while she paced the kitchen, a slim figure clad in jeans and a sweater and workmanlike boots. 'Look, I've got a few things to check outside. I might as well keep busy until Cesare arrives.'

'What sort of a name is that he has?' Brian Whitaker scoffed.

Lizzie dealt the older man an impatient glance as she put on her jacket because he had no excuse to be needling her or disparaging Cesare. But everything, she told herself in an urgent little pep talk, was *good* in her world. Chrissie had returned to university and soon she and her father would no longer need to worry about rent rises and bank debts they couldn't cover. 'It's an Italian name, just like mine and Chrissie's and Mum's and it's completely normal. Let's not forget that Cesare is about to wave a magic wand over our lives.'

'Even the Garden of Eden had the serpent,' her father countered with a curl of his lip and his usual determination to have the last word.

Lizzie drank in the fresh air with relief and walked to the stone wall bounding the yard to check the sheep in the field. Lambing hadn't started yet but it wouldn't be long before it did. If she had to leave home before then, Andrew would probably take the ewes, she was reasoning in the detached state of mind she had forged to keep herself calm since she had sent that text to Cesare. There were no successes without losses, no gains without costs and consequences. In the middle of that sobering reflection while she watched the lane for a car arriving, she heard a noise in the sky and she flung her head back in the fading light to look up.

A helicopter was coming in over the valley. As she watched it circled the top of the hill and swooped down low to come closer and then noisily hover. For a split second, Lizzie was frozen to the spot, unable to believe that the helicopter was actually planning to land in a field with stock in it. The craft's powerful lights splayed over the flock of fast-scattering sheep, which ran in a total panic down the hill. Lizzie ran for the gate, Archie at her heels, and flew over it like a high jumper while shouting instructions to her dog to retrieve the flock.

Heart pounding, she ran down the hill at breakneck speed but was still not fast enough to prevent the sheep from scrambling in a frantic escape over the wall at the foot and streaming across the next field towards the river. Sick with apprehension, she clambered over the wall and ran even faster while watching as Archie herded the frightened ewes away from the water's edge. The noise from the helicopter unluckily intensified at that point because the pilot was taking off again and the sheep herded close together and then took off terrified again in all directions.

Someone shouted her name and she was relieved to see Andrew Brook racing down the hill to join her. Struggling desperately to catch her breath, while wondering anxiously where Archie had disappeared to, she hurried on towards the riverbank to see if any of the animals had gone into the water. Andrew got there first and she saw him stooping down in the mud over something, whistling for his sheepdog. One of the sheep had got hurt in the commotion, she assumed, hurrying down to join him.

'I'm so sorry, Lizzie. He's hurt. He was too little to handle them in a panic like that,' Andrew told her.

Lizzie looked down in horror at the small prone body lying in the mud: it was Archie and he was whimpering. She knelt in the mud. *'Oh, no...'*

'I think it's only his leg that's broken but there could be internal injuries. He was trodden on,' Andrew, a stocky dark-haired man in his late twenties, reminded her.

'That *crazy* helicopter pilot! Are people insane?' Lizzie gasped, stricken, while Andrew, always resourceful, broke a small branch off a nearby tree, cut it to size with the knife in his pocket and splinted it to Archie's leg, wrapping it in place with twine.

'Nobody should land in a field with animals in it,' Andrew agreed. As Lizzie comforted her pet with a trembling hand he unfurled his mobile phone. 'We'd better get him to the vet. I'll ring ahead to warn Danny.'

Andrew's dog had retrieved the sheep and on the walk back uphill they were returned to the field from which they had fled. Lizzie was in shock and wildly dishevelled by the breakneck pace of her downhill marathon, sweat breaking on her brow, tears trickling down her cheeks as she held Archie's small, shivering body as gently as she could to her chest. Back in the yard, Lizzie went straight to the Land Rover and settled Archie on the front passenger seat.

'I'll come with you,' Andrew announced. 'I know how you feel about that daft dog.'

'Thanks but I can manage,' Lizzie assured him with a warm smile that acknowledged how comfortable she could still feel with her former boyfriend.

'That's the ex-fiancé—Andrew Brook, our neighbour,' Brian Whitaker informed Cesare, who was stationed beside him outside the back door of the cottage. 'They grew up together. I always thought they'd make a match of it but then he met Esther and married her instead.'

Cesare told himself that he had no desire for that information. He was already irritated that Lizzie hadn't been waiting to greet him—didn't she appreciate what a busy man he was? Now watching her smile beguilingly up at her ex-boyfriend, who was an attractive, stalwart six-footer, he was even less impressed. When she looked at the other man like that and squeezed his arm with easy intimacy it made him wonder why they had broken up and that dart of inappropriate curiosity set his even white teeth on edge, sending another wave of annoyance crashing through him.

'Lizzie!' her father called as Andrew strode back home across the couple of fields that separated their properties.

Lizzie turned her head and focused in bewilderment on the tall, darkly handsome male poised by her father's side. Her heartbeat suddenly thudded like a crack of doom in her ears and her throat tightened. Sheathed in an immaculate grey pinstripe business suit worn with a white shirt and scarlet tie, Cesare looked very much at odds with his surroundings but he still contrived to take her breath away and leave her mind briefly as blank as white paper. 'Good grief, when did you arrive? I didn't see a car.'

'I came in a helicopter...'

Lizzie, the Land Rover keys clenched tightly in one hand, froze. She blinked in fleeting bewilderment and then headed towards Cesare in a sudden movement, rage boiling up through the cracks of anxiety and concern for her dog and her flock. *'You're* the bloody idiot who let a helicopter land in a field full of stock?' she raked at him incredulously.

In all his life, nobody had ever addressed Cesare with such insolence. A faint frown line etched between his ebony brows, he stared at her as if he couldn't quite believe his ears. Indeed he was much more concerned with the reality that, in spite of her awareness of his visit, his bride-to-be still looked as though she had strayed in from a hostel for the homeless. A streak of dirt marred one cheekbone and her clothes were caked in mud and displaying damp patches. But when he glanced higher and saw the luminous colour in her cheeks that accentuated her hazel-green eyes and the contrast of that tumbling mane of admittedly messy white-blonde hair, he registered in some astonishment that even had she been wearing a bin liner it would not have dampened her physical appeal on his terms. His usual high standards, it seemed, were slipping.

'What's the problem?' Cesare enquired with perfect cool, reasoning that some sort of cultural misunderstanding could have provoked her sudden aggressive outburst.

'The problem is...'

'Don't shout at me,' Cesare sliced in softly. 'I am not hard of hearing.'

'Your pilot landed that helicopter in a field full of sheep...and he should be shot for it!' Lizzie framed rawly. 'They were so terrified they fled. All of them are pregnant, only days off lambing. If any of them miscarry after that crazed stampede, I'll be holding *you* responsible!'

For a fraction of a second, Cesare recalled the pilot striving to persuade him to land a couple of fields away but the prospect of a time-wasting muddy trek to the cottage had exasperated him and he had insisted on being set down as close as possible to his destination. 'The mistake was mine, not the pilot's. I chose the landing spot,' Cesare admitted, startling her with that confession. 'I know nothing about farming or the care of animals. Naturally I will compensate you and your father for any loss of income that results.'

'Well, the man can't say fairer than that,' Brian Whitaker cut in, sending his furious daughter a warning glance. 'Let that be the end of it.'

'Archie was *hurt*!' Lizzie protested fierily, shooting Cesare a seething look that warned him that even admitting his mistake was insufficient to soothe her. 'The flock trampled him at the river. I'm taking him to the vet now for emergency treatment and I haven't got the time…or the patience…to deal with you!'

Cesare watched in disbelief as his future bride unlocked the rusty vehicle several feet away and began to climb in.

'You've done it now. She treats that stupid dog like her firstborn!' Brian Whitaker muttered impatiently and retreated back indoors, bowing out of the situation.

With the split-second timing that matched Cesare's lightning-fast intellect, he strode forward and opened the passenger door of the Land Rover to take the only step left open to him. 'I'll accompany you to the vet's,' he informed her flatly.

Very much disconcerted by that announcement, Lizzie flicked him a frowning appraisal. 'You'll have to hold Archie.'

Cesare, so far out of his comfort zone that he already felt as if he were trapped in something of a nightmare, finally noticed that it was a two-seat vehicle and that the scruffy dog lay comatose on the only seat available for his own use.

Lizzie leapt back out of the car. 'I'll move him and *then* you can get in,' she told him, racing round the back of the vehicle to scoop up Archie in trembling hands and usher him in.

'I could drive,' Cesare pointed out drily.

'You don't know where you're going and I know where the potholes are,' Lizzie told him incomprehensibly as she very gently rested Archie down on Cesare's lap. 'Please make sure he doesn't fall.'

Tears were choking Lizzie's throat. Archie was so quiet and he had never been a quiet dog. Right at that very minute, he could be *dying*, his brave little life and loving spirit ebbing away, and that was why she wasn't going to waste time arguing with Cesare Sabatino about anything.

'Is he still breathing?' Lizzie demanded, turning out onto the road.

'I can feel his heart beating,' Cesare proffered quietly, blocking out his uneasy awareness that the vehicle stank of animals and was far from clean. He stroked the still body for want of anything else to do and was startled when the dog twisted his head to lick at his hand.

'He trusts you,' Lizzie informed him.

'He doesn't have much choice in the matter,' Cesare fielded, reckoning that he had been sent to Yorkshire solely to suffer. In his opinion she drove like a maniac. He had spent the day travelling and his day had started at six in the morning in Geneva. Now it was eight in the evening and, not only had he not eaten for hours, but he was also convinced that many more hours would pass before he could even hope for the opportunity. He knew she had no idea that he had planned to take her out to dinner and, since he didn't have a woolly fleece and cloven hooves, it would never occur to Lizzie to feed him.

Unaware of her unwelcome passenger's thoughts, Lizzie rammed the Land Rover to an abrupt jolting halt in a small car park. Carefully carrying Archie, Lizzie stalked into the surgery, leaving Cesare, a male who was unaccustomed to being ignored, to follow her. An older man greeted them and carried the dog off to be X-rayed, leaving Lizzie and Cesare in the small, dull waiting room.

In consternation, Cesare watched Lizzie fighting off tears again. Driven by a desperate masculine urge to shift her thoughts to what he viewed as more positive issues, he murmured, 'So, we're getting married?'

Lizzie marvelled at his lack of compassion and understanding. Did he really think she was in any frame of mind to discuss that while she was waiting to hear whether Archie would live or die? 'Yes, but it won't really be a marriage,' she parried, striving not to look at him because he really had the most stunning dark golden eyes and every time she looked she ended up staring and she didn't want him to notice her behaving like a silly schoolgirl.

'We're not going for gold, then,' Cesare assumed, referring to the requirement for a child in the will while surveying her down-bent head with a sense of deep dissatisfaction that took him aback. Why was he feeling that way? Common sense suggested that he should settle for taking Athene for a visit to Lionos and think himself lucky to have gained that much from the exchange.

A tangle of silvery hair brushed the delicate cheekbones of Lizzie's heart-shaped face and she glanced up through the silken veil of her lashes, green eyes clear and direct. 'Well, yes, we are. I've thought of a way round that.'

'There's no way round it,' Cesare informed her impatiently, marvelling at the luminous quality of those tear-drenched eyes.

'AI,' she declared quietly.

His straight ebony brows lifted. 'AI?'

'Artificial insemination. We use it with the

stock and we can do it that way too,' Lizzie muttered in an undertone, trying not to succumb to discomfiture because he was *really* staring at her now as if he had never heard of such a process. 'I mean, that way there's no need at all for us to get up close and personal. We can both conserve our dignity.'

Cesare was staggered by the suggestion. 'Dignity?' he queried thinly, his first reaction being one of male offence until his clever brain examined the suggestion. For him, it would be a win-win situation, he acknowledged grudgingly. He would not have to sacrifice his freedom in any field because the marriage would be a detached charade from start to finish. That *was* the civilised sensible approach because there would always be the risk that sexual involvement could muddy the waters of their arrangement. But while his intellect reinforced that rational outlook, he discovered that he was curiously reluctant to embrace the concept of a child fathered in a lab rather than in the normal way and equally reluctant to accept that Lizzie Whitaker would never share his bed.

'Well, obviously neither one of us would want to be put in the position where we would have to have sex with a stranger.'

Without warning, unholy amusement burnished Cesare's lean, darkly handsome features. 'I don't think you know much about the average male.'

Colour flared like a banner in Lizzie's cheeks. 'And if that's the sort of man you are, I don't think you should be boasting about it!' she snapped pointedly.

Cesare breathed in slow and deep and resisted the urge to ask her if she ever lightened up. It was something of a shock for him to discover that there was a woman alive utterly impervious to his looks and charisma. He didn't believe in false modesty and had been well aware since the teen years that he could attract women in droves, a success rating that had only been enhanced by his gradual rise to billionaire status. Lizzie, however, put out no encouraging vibes and was not remotely flirtatious.

Watching the cool forbidding expression spread across his lean bronzed face, Lizzie took fright and said, 'I'm sorry…I'm too worried about Archie to mind what I say. I didn't intend to be rude but you must understand that two people with as little in common as we have really do need a get-out clause when it comes to having a baby,' she framed with a shy upward glance. 'And if I agree to that, there would be additional safeguards I would require.'

'Such as?'

Lizzie breathed in deep. 'You would have to agree to take on the role of acting as a father to the child until it grew up. Obviously we'll marry and then divorce…whenever.' Lizzie shifted an uncertain hand. 'But a child has specific needs from a parent and those needs must be met with love and security from *both* of us. That would be quite a responsibility for you to take on for the next twenty years and I need to be sure that you're willing to accept that.'

A very faint darkening of colour across Cesare's spectacular cheekbones highlighted his discomfiture. He had assumed that Lizzie was planning to discuss the financial rewards for her willingness to fulfil the terms of the will and her true, infinitely more responsible and caring angle of interest had pierced him with a rare sense of guilt. 'Why are you so willing to take on that responsibility?' he prompted.

'I've always wanted a child of my own,' Lizzie responded, quite comfortable and secure in making that admission. 'But I don't really want a man to go *with* the child, so the arrangement you suggested would probably suit me best of all. At the same time I don't want to raise a fatherless child, so an occasional father such as you would be is even more acceptable.'

Cesare was quietly stunned by those statements. The women he socialised with were never so frank about a desire to conceive either now or in the future. He wondered if she was still in love with her ex or simply some sort of man-hater because it was unusual for so young a woman to decide that she wanted to live her life alone. And then in dawning dismay he heard himself say, 'Are you gay?'

Lizzie turned bright pink but recognised why he had interpreted her words in that light. 'No, that's not the problem,' she responded stiffly, determined to keep her reasons for her solitary choice of lifestyle strictly private. There was no requirement whatsoever for her to explain herself to him and she was grateful for the fact.

'If we had a child together, I would hope to meet all your expectations of a father,' Cesare informed her with quiet conviction. 'As it happens, I have a very good father of my own and appreciate the importance of the role he plays.'

Lizzie nodded. 'That was my only real concern… Oh.' She hesitated but there was no way of avoiding the most pressing requirement. 'If we're to proceed with this I'm afraid I'll need some money from you upfront. I have to be honest—we are all stony broke. My sister needs some cash to stay on at university and I'll have to rent a property in the village for my dad because when I leave, he'll be relinquishing the tenancy of the farm.'

Absorbing the fluctuating expressions of embarrassment and apprehension skimming her heart-shaped face, Cesare sent her a soothing smile. 'Naturally it's not a problem. I expected something of the sort.'

'You knew how we were fixed…*before* you visited?' Lizzie queried in surprise.

'I never enter a situation blind,' Cesare countered unapologetically.

Danny the vet appeared in the doorway. 'Archie will be out in a minute. My nurse is just finishing up with him. His leg's broken and he's had a blow to the skull, which means he's a little woozy, but other than that he seems fine.'

After the vet had explained his treatment

and proffered medication for the coming days, Archie emerged in the nurse's arms, a cast attached to one small leg and a balloon collar round his neck to prevent him from nibbling at it. Lizzie gathered him close, tears tripping from her eyes again as she huskily thanked the older man while Cesare insisted on taking care of the bill.

'I'm very attached to Archie,' Lizzie explained, dashing tears of relief from her eyes with her elbow. 'You can drive back if you want. The keys are in my pocket.'

Cesare fished out the keys and unlocked the car. 'I was hoping you would fly back to London with me tonight.'

'Tonight?' Lizzie exclaimed in disbelief. 'That's impossible!'

'We have a tight time schedule. I have everything arranged. Is it really impossible?' Cesare prompted drily. 'You appear to have no presentable clothes and can't need to pack much.'

'But I have to sort out somewhere for Dad to live and move him out of the cottage.'

'I have staff who will hire professionals to deal with those tasks for you,' Cesare told her with complete cool. 'You've had your say.

I have agreed to your terms and now I need you to come to London.'

It was bite-the-bullet time, Lizzie registered, angrily colliding with brilliant dark eyes as hard as jet. He was being unreasonable. Surely there was no excuse for such haste? But what choice did she have? The arrangement having been agreed, he was now in charge of events. 'I'll have to call in with my neighbour to ask him to look after the flock.'

'Andrew Brook?'

Lizzie stiffened. 'Yes.'

'Why did you break up?'

'That's private,' Lizzie told him waspishly.

Cesare gritted his teeth. 'We'll go and see him now, so that you can make your preparations.'

Lizzie left Archie asleep in the Land Rover. Esther opened the door and her look of dismay mortified Lizzie, although she had always been aware that Andrew's last-minute exchange of would-be wives had caused Esther almost as much heartache and humiliation as it had caused Lizzie. People had condemned Esther for sleeping with a man who was engaged to another woman. They had judged her even harder for falling pregnant and thereby forcing the affair into the open and some locals had ignored Esther ever since.

Andrew sprang up from the kitchen table while Lizzie carried out introductions whereupon Cesare startled her by taking charge. 'Lizzie and I are leaving for London tonight— we're getting married,' he explained. 'Lizzie wants to know if you'll take her sheep.'

Lizzie saw the surprise and relief darting across Esther's face and looked away again, her own colour high. Esther would be glad to see her leave the neighbourhood and she didn't feel she could really blame the other woman for that, not after the way people had treated her.

'This is a surprise and it calls for a celebration,' Andrew pronounced with genuine pleasure. 'I didn't even know you were seeing anyone, Lizzie.'

Home-made peach wine was produced. Cesare found it sickly sweet but he appreciated the sentiment while he watched and read his companions and made certain interesting deductions. Andrew Brook appeared fond of Lizzie but no more than that. Indeed his every look of warmth was for his wife, who was a rather plain, plump young woman who couldn't hold a candle to Lizzie in the looks department. Lizzie, on the other hand, Cesare could not read at all. She chatted but was clearly eager to leave as soon as was polite.

'Are you planning to enlighten me yet?' Cesare drawled when they returned to the Land Rover, his Italian accent licking round the edges of every syllable in the sexiest way imaginable.

Lizzie was bitterly amused by that stray thought when she didn't do sex or even know what sexy was. That had lain at the heart of her disastrous relationship with Andrew when she had learned that she was simply one of those women who did not like to be touched. She had assumed—*wrongly*—when she agreed to marry him that her own response would naturally change as time went on and they became closer. But that hadn't happened and her feelings hadn't changed.

'Andrew had an affair with Esther while we were engaged and she got pregnant. We broke up six weeks before our wedding day and he married her the following month. They're very happy together,' Lizzie explained flatly. 'That means I've got an unused wedding gown in my wardrobe, so I'll bring that down to London.'

'*No!*' Cesare sliced in with innate distaste. 'I will buy you another dress.'

'But that's silly and wasteful when there's no need for it!' Lizzie reasoned in bafflement.

'If we are trying to persuade my family that this is a genuine marriage, you will need a designer gown with all the usual trimmings.'

'But how could anyone possibly believe it was genuine? We're chalk and cheese and we only just met.'

'You'll be enjoying a full makeover in London and only my father knows when we first met. By the time I'm finished with you, they *will* believe, *cara*,' Cesare insisted.

'And what if I don't want a makeover?'

'If you want to be convincing in the role you're being paid to take, you don't have a choice,' Cesare told her softly. Of course she wanted a makeover, he thought grimly, unconvinced by her show of reluctance. She was willing to do just about anything for money. Hadn't she already demonstrated the fact? She was prepared to become a mother simply to sell the island to him. But then to be fair, he acknowledged, he was willing to become a father to buy Lionos although, in his case, he had additional and far more presentable motives.

What was the use of working so hard when he had no heir to follow him? What easier way could he acquire a child to inherit his empire? He had seen too many marriages explode into the bitterness and division of divorce, heard too many stories about children traumatised by their parents splitting up. The will had given him a chance to avoid that kind of fallout *and* the imprisonment of taking 'for ever after' vows with one woman. A marriage that was a marriage only on paper and a child born prior to a low-key civilised divorce would suit Cesare's needs very nicely indeed.

Out of Cesare's response, only one phrase assailed Lizzie: *you're being paid*. It was an unwelcome but timely reminder and she chewed at her full lower lip, restraining a tart response. Hopefully within a couple of months he would have no further use for her and she would get her life back and, even more hopefully, a life that would stretch to include the sheer joy of becoming a mother for the first time. When that time came, maybe she would be able to find some sort of work training course and accommodation near Chrissie. Or maybe that was a bad idea, she reflected uneasily, suspecting that her sibling had the right to her independence without a big sister hovering protectively somewhere nearby.

'A moment before we go inside...' Cesare breathed, striding round the bonnet of the rusty farm vehicle.

A frown drew Lizzie's brows together as she hovered by the back door. When he reached out and tugged her close, Lizzie was so taken aback that she simply froze. His hands came up to frame her cheekbones and she gazed up into glittering golden eyes that reflected the lights shining out from the farmhouse windows, her nostrils flaring on the faint fresh scent of his cologne and the underlying hint of clean, fresh man.

At that point while she was mulling over why he smelled so good to her, Cesare lowered his proud dark head and kissed her. Lizzie stopped breathing in shock, electrified by the sensation and taste of his firm sensual mouth on hers with her heart hammering and her pulse racing as if she were riding a Big Dipper at an amusement park. He nibbled her lower lip and thunder crashed in her ears, the earth literally moving when he swiped his tongue along her full lower lip in an erotic flick that made her quiver like a jelly.

Forbidden warmth burst into being inside her, swelling her breasts, tightening her nipples, spearing down between her legs in a twin assault on her senses. A hard urgency now laced the passionate pressure of his mouth on hers and her head fell back, lips parting by instinct to welcome the deeply sensual dart of his tongue. He pulled her closer, welding her to every powerful line of his lean, powerfully masculine body with a big hand splayed across her hips to hold her in place and in spite of their clothing she felt his arousal, the hard, unmistakeable ridge between them. With almost superhuman force of will because she was on the edge of panic, Lizzie pressed her hand against his shoulder to push him back from her and, to be fair to him, he freed her immediately.

'That's enough,' she framed unevenly, her breath rasping in her tight throat as an ache of what she knew could only be dissatisfaction spread at the heart of her. 'Why the heck did you do that?'

'If we intend to fool people into crediting that we are a genuine couple, we have to be able to behave like a couple...at least, occasionally,' Cesare delivered with an audibly ragged hitch in his breathing.

'I don't like being touched,' Lizzie told him in a small flat voice.

You could've fooled me, Cesare thought in disbelief, still tasting the sweetness of her soft, lush lips and struggling to suppress the rush of hungry excitement that had lit him up like a burning torch.

She was out of bounds, he reminded himself stubbornly. He was not planning to bed her. She didn't want it and *he* didn't want it either. Regrettably his body was out of step with his brain, though, and somehow she exuded all the allure of a juicy hamburger to a very reluctant vegetarian. But, Cesare reminded himself stubbornly, he could get sex anywhere. He had Celine for uncommitted sexual satisfaction. He wasn't about to risk screwing up his marital arrangement with Lizzie by flirting with that kind of intimacy. It would blur the boundaries and she might start behaving like a real wife and even start thinking that she could attach strings to him.

'So, it was just a sort of test?' Lizzie gathered in relief, assuming that it was an approach that was unlikely to be repeated very often.

'You won the gold medal for excellence, *bella mia,*' Cesare quipped, striving to will his libido back down to a manageable level but that was a challenge while all he could think about, all he could see in his head, was Lizzie spread across a bed, stark naked and not only willing but also wild. The imagery didn't help, nor did it help that he knew he, who prided himself on his detachment in business situations, was indulging in a deeply improbable but very male fantasy.

Two hours later, Lizzie was seated in a limousine with Cesare in silence. Her case was stowed, Archie was asleep on her knee and Cesare was working on his laptop. She was still thinking about that kiss, wondering what magic spark Cesare had that Andrew had so conspicuously lacked. Was it truly just a case of physical chemistry?

Frustration filled Lizzie to overflowing. There had been very few men in her life, very few kisses and she was still a virgin. Andrew had repulsed her, yet he was a young, attractive man and she had loved him. Naturally, she had assumed that she simply wasn't a very sexual woman. But within seconds of Cesare kissing her, fireworks had gone off inside her in a rush of excitement unlike anything she had ever felt. And now, for the very first time in her life, she was studying a powerful masculine thigh and the distinctive bulge at the crotch and wondering what a man looked like naked. Colour washed in a veil to her hairline and she studied Archie instead, fondling a shaggy ear as the dog slept.

It was sexual curiosity, that was all. Silly, immature, she labelled with growing embarrassment, but nothing to really worry about. After all, nothing was going to happen with Cesare. And as for that moment of panic in his arms? One kiss and she imagined she was about to tumble into an adolescent infatuation as easily as her mother had once done? No, she was much too sensible for that, she told herself soothingly. Cesare was gorgeous and well-off and arrogant and he probably slept around as such men reputedly did. He was not her type at all...

Absolutely *not* his type, Cesare was reflecting with satisfaction. One dynamite kiss didn't alter the fact that she dressed like a bag lady, had poor manners and barely a feminine bone in her body. Or that she treated him rather like a lost umbrella someone had left behind on a train seat...

CHAPTER FOUR

THE MAKEOVER, ALONG with the shopping and the ultra-grooming at a very fancy beauty salon, shook Lizzie to her very depths.

She was transformed and she knew it and was surprised by how very much better it made her feel to see herself polished to glossiness, with that awful brown dye gone from the last few inches of her pale silvery hair. Every time she had seen that dye in the mirror it had reminded her of Andrew and the bad times, so it was a relief to be finally rid of it and stop wondering if he ironically had tried to change *her* into Esther, who had mud-brown hair of no great distinction. She regarded her long, glittery nails with positive girlish delight because she had never known such beauty tweaking could transform her work-roughened hands. The calluses were gone as well, her entire skin surface buffed and moisturised to perfection. There was no doubt about it: it made her feel like a new woman, a woman of greater assurance than she had been when she first slunk through the doors of the salon, feeling like a crime against femininity in her untouched, unpolished state.

How would Cesare view her now?

Her cheeks flushed at the thought. Why should that matter to her? What was his opinion worth? Presumably without the polishing he wouldn't have wanted to be seen out with her in public and that was a lowering reflection, she acknowledged ruefully. She had been transformed and she appreciated it, best not to think too deeply beyond that, she decided wryly. And now all dressed up to the nines she felt more armoured to cope with the hen party ahead even if it was without the support of her sister.

Sadly, Chrissie had an exam the next day and there was absolutely no way she could join Lizzie and Cesare's sisters. Lizzie was disappointed. She liked Cesare's friendly siblings very much but they were still strangers and somewhat more uncomfortably, strangers she had to keep a front up with. They thought it was a normal wedding with a bride and groom in love and happy. Unfortunately, living up to that false expectation was a strain even on a shopping and beauty trip.

'You mean, you really *aren't* pregnant?' Sofia, Cesare's youngest half-sister, gasped as she watched Lizzie down a vodka cocktail with every sign of enjoyment. 'Cesare told us you weren't but we didn't believe him.'

'This conversation is not happening,' Paola groaned in apology, the eldest of the trio of sisters, a teacher and married woman and rather more circumspect than her single, fun-loving sisters in what she chose to say. 'I'm so sorry, Lizzie.'

Lizzie smiled, masking her loneliness and chagrin. 'It's all right. I'm not offended. I know you're surprised that your brother's getting married in such a hurry—'

'When we never thought he'd get married at all,' his third half-sister Maurizia slotted in frankly.

'Obviously he's nuts about you!' Sofia giggled. 'That's the only explanation that makes sense. When I sent him that photo of you all dressed up to go out tonight, he wasted no time telling me that he wanted you to stay at home and that he saw no reason for you to have a hen night.'

Of course Cesare didn't see any reason, Lizzie reflected ruefully, glugging her drink because she didn't know what to say to his very accepting and loveable sisters or indeed to his pleasant stepmother, Ottavia, none of whom had a clue that the wedding wasn't the real thing. She had guessed, however, that his father, Goffredo, was simply playing along with their pretence but she found that same pretence stressful and knew it was why she was drinking so much and living on her nerves. Luckily Cesare had not been required to put on much of an act, she conceded resentfully, as he had taken refuge in his city apartment, after marooning her in his unbelievably luxurious town house with his family, before flying off to New York on urgent business.

Apparently it was the norm for Cesare to move out of his flashy and huge town house into his exclusive city apartment when his family arrived for a visit. Lizzie had found that strange but his family did not, joking that Cesare had always liked his own space and avoided anything that might take his main focus off business, which evidently involved socialising with his family as well. Lizzie thought that was sad but had kept her opinion tactfully to herself.

He was *so* rich: in spite of the limo and the driver and the helicopter, she had had no idea *how* rich her future fake husband was. Lizzie was still in shock from travelling in a private jet and walking into a house the size of a palace with over ten en-suite bedrooms and innumerable staff. She had then done what she should have done a week earlier and had checked him out on the Internet, learning that he was the head of a business mega-empire and more in the billionaire than the multimillionaire category.

Indeed the house, followed by the experience of being literally engulfed by his gregarious family, had only been the first of the culture shocks rattling Lizzie's security on its axis. Two solid days of clothes shopping followed by a physical head-to-toe makeover had left its mark. For that reason it was hardly surprising that she should be at last enjoying the chance to relax and have a few drinks in good company for the first time in more years than she cared to count.

Seated on his jet, furiously checking his watch to calculate the landing time, Cesare enlarged the photograph on his tablet and scrutinised it with lingering disbelief.

Don't you dare take Lizzie out dressed like that to a club! he had texted his half-sister Maurizia, with a confusing mix of anger, frustration and concern assailing him in a dark flood of reactions that made him uncomfortable to the extreme.

He still couldn't take his eyes off the photograph: Lizzie smiling as he had never seen her and sheathed in an emerald-green, 'barely there', strappy short dress with perilous high heels on her shapely legs. It was an amazing transformation. A magic wand had been waved over the bag lady. She looked fantastic and would outshine every woman around her now that her natural beauty had been polished up and brought to the fore. Her glorious mane of hair had been restored as he'd instructed, *not* cut. It gleamed in a silken tumble of silver strands round her delicately pointed face, green eyes huge, pouty mouth lush and pink. Cesare swore under his breath, outraged by his sisters' interference and the hen-party nonsense. Lizzie was no more fit to be let loose in a London nightclub than a toddler and now he would have to go and retrieve her!

* * *

'You're not supposed to be here… This is *her* night!' one of his sisters carolled accusingly as soon as he arrived at the women's table.

'Where is she?' Cesare ground out, unamused, while he scanned the dance floor.

Looking daggers at her big brother, Sofia shifted a reluctant hand to show him. 'Don't spoil her night. She's having a whale of a time!'

Cesare centred his incredulous dark gaze on the sight of his bride-to-be, a pink hen-night sash diagonally dissecting her slender, shapely body as she danced, arms raised, silvery hair flying, feet moving in time to the fast beat. What infuriated him was the sight of the two men trying to attract her attention because she appeared to be dancing in a world of her own. Suddenly Lizzie teetered to a stop, clearly dizzy as she swayed on her very high heels. With a suppressed snarl of annoyance, Cesare, ignoring his siblings' wide-eyed disbelief at his behaviour, stalked across the floor to hastily settle steadying hands on Lizzie's slim shoulders.

'Cesare…' Lizzie proclaimed with a wide, sunny smile because it only took one lingering glance to remind her how tall, dark and sleekly gorgeous he was. He towered over her, lean bronzed face shadowed and hollowed by the flickering lights that enhanced his spectacular bone structure, stunning dark golden eyes intent on her. She was really, *really* pleased to see him, a familiar reassuring image in a new world that was unnervingly different and unsettling. In fact for a split second she almost succumbed to a deeply embarrassing urge to hug him. Then, luckily remembering that hugging wasn't part of their deal, she restrained herself.

'You're drunk,' his perfectly shaped mouth framed, destroying the effect of his reassuring presence.

'Of course I'm not drunk!' Lizzie slurred, throwing up her hands in emphasis only to brace them on his broad chest while she wondered why her legs wanted to splay like a newborn calf's trying to walk for the first time.

'You are,' Cesare repeated flatly.

'I'm *not*,' Lizzie insisted, holding onto his forearms to stay upright, her shoe soles still displaying a worrying urge to slide across the floor of their own volition.

'I'm taking you home,' Cesare mouthed as the deafening music crashed all around them.

'I'm not ready to go home yet!' she shouted at him.

Lizzie couldn't work out what Cesare said in answer to that declaration. His deep-set eyes glittered like banked-down fires in his lean, strong face and he had bent down and lifted her up into his arms before she could even begin to guess his intention.

'Think we're going home,' Lizzie informed his sisters forlornly from the vantage point of his arms as he paused by their table.

'You *didn't* look after her!' Cesare growled at one of his sisters, in answer to whatever comment had been made.

'What am I? A dog or a child?' Lizzie demanded, staring up at him, noticing that he needed a shave because a heavy five o'clock shadow outlined his lower jawline, making it seem even harder and more aggressive than usual. It framed his wide, sensual mouth though, drawing attention to the perfectly sculpted line of his lips. He kissed like a dream, she recalled abstractedly, wondering when he'd do it again.

'Think we should kiss so that your sisters believe we're a *real* couple?' Lizzie asked him winningly.

'If we were real, I'd strangle you, *cara*,'

Cesare countered without hesitation. 'I leave you alone for three days and I come back and you're going crazy on the dance floor and getting blind drunk.'

'*Not* drunk,' Lizzie proclaimed stubbornly.

Cesare rolled his eyes and with scant ceremony stuffed her in the back of the waiting limousine. 'Lie down before you fall over.'

'You're so smug,' Lizzie condemned and closed her eyes because the interior of the limousine was telescoping around her in the most peculiar way.

Cesare consoled himself with the hope that such behaviour was not a warning sign of things to come. How could he blame her for wanting some fun? He had a very good idea of what life must have been like for her on that farm with her misery of a father, always there at her elbow, keen to remind her of every mistake and failure. For the very first time in his life he realised just how lucky he had been with Goffredo, who saw everything through rose-tinted, forgiving spectacles. In comparison, Brian Whitaker's view of life was seriously depressing.

Lizzie opened her eyes. 'Do you want to kiss me?' she enquired.

Cesare skimmed his disconcerted gaze to

her animated features, taking in the playful grin she wore. 'Do you *want* me to kiss you?'

Lizzie flushed and shifted on the seat. 'You're not supposed to ask that.'

'You expect me to act like a caveman?'

Lizzie thought about that. She had rather enjoyed being carried out of the club. Was that weird? She scolded herself for that enjoyment while mustering up a dim memory of her mother giggling and tossing her hair, eyes sparkling at the latest man in her life. Inwardly she cringed a little from the comparison she saw.

'Only when you're sober and you know what you're doing,' Cesare extended infuriatingly.

'You believe I could only want to kiss you when I'm drunk?'

Cesare suppressed a groan and studied her. If truth be told, it would take very little encouragement for him to flatten her along the back seat and take inexcusable advantage of her delightfully feminine body. 'We have a business arrangement,' he reminded her doggedly, cursing the hot swell of the erection disturbing his poise because just the thought of doing anything to her turned him on hard and fast.

Her honey-brown lashes flickered. 'I'm open to negotiation.'

'*No*, you're not,' Cesare informed her grimly, lean bronzed face set in forbidding lines, mobile mouth compressed. 'There will be absolutely no negotiation on that score tonight.'

Was it so wrong, Lizzie asked herself, that she should want to experience just once what other women commonly experienced? She had always wanted to be normal, to *feel* normal. Was that wrong? Indecent? Her cheeks burned. Naturally she had picked him. *That* kiss... Somehow he had become her forbidden object of desire. How had that happened? Treacherous heat curling in her pelvis, Lizzie breathed in slow and deep.

Cesare watched her feathery lashes dip and the sound of her breathing slow as she slid into a doze. Well, he wouldn't be letting her loose around alcohol again. Sex, drink and business arrangements did not make for a rational or successful combination. And he was a *very* rational guy, wasn't he? Here he was being a saint and protecting her from doing something she would regret. Or would she? he wondered with inbred cynicism. She was a gold-digger, after all, and sure to be on a

high after the orgy of spending that had centred on her in recent days.

He was acting against his own nature,
he acknowledged grudgingly. In reality, he
wanted to fall on her like a sex-starved sailor
on shore leave and keep her awake all night.
Instead he was likely to spend half the night
in a cold shower. He should have made more
of an effort to see Celine. Clearly, it was the
lack of regular sex that was playing merry
hell with his hormones.

Lizzie awakened as Cesare half walked,
half carried her into the town house only to
stop dead as Goffredo and his stepmother, Ottavia, appeared in the doorway of the drawing room.

'Your daughters are still partying,' Cesare
announced. 'Lizzie was falling asleep, so I
brought her home early.'

'Cesare is a party pooper,' Lizzie framed
with difficulty.

Goffredo grinned and Ottavia chuckled
and the older couple vanished back into the
drawing room.

At the foot of the stairs, Cesare abandoned
the pretence that Lizzie could walk unaided
and swept her up into his arms.

'I like it when you do this,' Lizzie told him. 'It's so…so…masculine.'

'We are lucky you don't weigh more,' Cesare quipped, barely out of breath as they reached the top of the stairs.

A sudden lurch in the stomach region made Lizzie tense and she crammed a stricken hand to her mouth, mumbling, 'Cesare…'

To give him his due, Cesare was not slow on the uptake and he strode through the nearest door at speed and deposited her in a bathroom.

Lizzie was ingloriously ill. He pushed her hair out of the way, gave her a cloth, extended a toothbrush, which he unwrapped, and politely ignored her repetitive apologies for her behaviour. When she couldn't stand up again, he removed her shoes for her and supported her over to the sink.

'I don't make a habit of this,' she declared, rinsing her mouth several times over while hanging onto the vanity unit.

'I should hope not, *bellezza mia.*'

'What does that mean? The Italian bit?'

And he told her that it meant 'my beauty'.

'But that's a downright lie,' she protested, studying her bleary-eyed reflection in dismay. The make-up girl's artistry and the hairdresser's skill were no longer apparent in the flushed face, smudged eyeliner and tousled hair she now saw in the mirror.

'You need to lie down,' Cesare asserted, lifting her again so that the bathroom spun and then the bedroom that followed.

Lizzie lay flat and dead still on the bed, afraid to move lest her surroundings began revolving again. 'Where's Archie? I want Archie.'

'Archie stays downstairs.' Cesare reminded her of the household rule, announced by Primo, his imperturbable manservant, on the day she moved in.

'But that's just mean… He always sleeps with me,' she mumbled.

Cesare almost groaned out loud. She lay splayed across his bed, clearly trusting him when he didn't trust himself because she was displaying a wanton amount of bare slender thigh.

'If I can't have Archie for company, I'll have you,' Lizzie muttered. 'Lie down.'

Cesare snatched up the phone and issued a terse instruction. Within the space of a minute, Primo arrived at the door with Archie. Cesare clasped Archie and carried him over to the bed, whereupon the dog curled up obediently at Lizzie's feet with his head resting across her ankles.

'You should get into bed…you can't sleep in your clothes,' Cesare told her.

'Why not?'

Cesare released his breath in an exasperated hiss and came down on the bed beside her to run her zip down.

'What are you doing?' she whispered curiously as he smoothed the straps of the dress down off her slim shoulders.

'Making you more comfortable.' Business arrangement, *business* arrangement, bloody business arrangement, Cesare was dutifully repeating inside his head as he eased her out of the dress to expose a filmy and provocative bra and panties set in turquoise lace. He wasn't looking, he wasn't reacting, he told himself doggedly while his dark golden gaze clung of its own volition to the surprisingly full, plump curves swelling the lace cups, revealing pale pink nipples that made his mouth water and the shadowy vee at her crotch. He yanked the sheet over Lizzie's prone length so fast that she rolled and, having been disturbed and crammed in below the sheet without warning, Archie also loosed a whimper of complaint.

Lizzie stretched out a searching hand, her eyes closed. The room was going round and round and round behind her lowered eyelids and she felt lost and nauseous. 'Where you going?'

Weary after a day spent travelling and his last-minute sprint to deal with Lizzie, Cesare surrendered to the obvious. If he left her alone, might she wander off? Sleep on the floor? Have an accident? Stumble into the wrong bedroom? And what if she was sick again? 'I'm not going anywhere.' He stripped down to his boxers and lay down on the other side of the bed. A small, callused hand closed over the thumb of his right hand and held on tight. He wasn't used to sharing a bed and he liked his own space.

Lizzie settled up against a warm solid shape while Archie tunnelled below the sheet to settle down by a less restive set of feet.

Lizzie wakened with a desperate thirst at some timeless hour of the night while it was still dark. She slid her feet off the side of the bed, her soles finding the floor, and slowly straightened. A wave of dizziness immediately engulfed her and she compressed her lips hard, sober enough now to be furious with herself. Despite having hardly eaten all day she had foolishly downed all that alcohol and got carried away by the party atmosphere. Suppressing a groan of frustration, she fumbled for the switch on the bedside light and then stared in bewilderment round the unfamiliar room before focusing on the male sharing the wide bed with her.

Cesare was half naked and lying on top of the sheet she had been lying beneath. He was beautifully built with a broad bronzed torso and corded abdomen that rippled with lean muscle. One long, powerful, hair-roughened thigh was partially raised, the other flat. Unshaven, he exuded a rough, edgy masculinity that made her breath hitch in her throat as she peered down at him in the lamplight. His lashes were like black silk fans and almost long enough to touch his amazing cheekbones.

She remembered asking him if he wanted to kiss her, absolutely angling for his attention, and she almost screamed out loud at that demeaning memory. She headed for the bathroom with hot cheeks and a frustrated sense of self-loathing and shame that she could have been so silly. Had she asked him to stay with her as well? For goodness' sake, it was obviously his bedroom and he had only brought

her there the night before because it was the
nearest option when she felt sick. Now he had
seen her in her underwear and she was mortified, although not as mortified as she would
have been had he removed that as well. Her
head throbbing, she drank about a gallon of
cold water and freshened up as best she could
without her own toiletries. She crept out of
the bathroom in search of something to wear
so that she could return to her own room.

Tiptoeing like a cat burglar, she opened the
door into a massive wardrobe and eased back
a sliding door to yank a man's white shirt off
a hanger. The bra was digging into her mid-
riff and she released the catch and removed
it and the panties, wondering if she dared go
for a shower. Donning the shirt, she rolled up
the sleeves and buttoned it.

Being around Cesare made her feel out of
control but was that so surprising? She hadn't
dated since Andrew, hadn't seen the point,
and before him there had only been a hand-
ful of unremarkable men. In recent times,
she had had no social outlets and had only
occasionally left the farm. It cost money to
socialise and there had been none to spare.
Being with Cesare's light-hearted sisters had
been so much fun that she had forgotten to

monitor how much she was drinking. One glimpse of Cesare when she was in that weakened condition had had the same effect on her as a hit man shooting her directly between the eyes. He was a very good-looking male, that was all. Noticing the fact simply meant she was female and alive and not that she wanted to pursue anything with him.

Hovering by the bed, Lizzie tried to work out how to get Archie out from below the sheet without either hurting him or waking Cesare.

'What are you doing?' Cesare husked as she yanked at the sheet to try and reach her dog. Blinking up at her with frowning dark eyes, he lifted a muscular arm to check the gold watch he still wore. '*Inferno!* It's three in the morning.'

'I should go back to my own room.'

'Don't wake up the whole household. Stay and go back to sleep,' Cesare advised her drily, flipping onto his side in a display of indifference that made her grit her teeth.

Would she wake anyone up? Stifling a sound of frustration, Lizzie doused the light and snaked back below the sheet.

Early morning was sending pale light through the blinds when she next surfaced, feeling considerably healthier than she had earlier but decidedly overheated. An arm was draped round her ribcage and she was locked intimately close to a very male body, a very *aroused* male body. A surge of heat that had nothing to do with his higher temperature pooled in Lizzie's pelvis. She eased over onto her back and looked up unwarily into heavily fringed eyes the colour of melted bronze. Her throat ran dry, her breathing ruptured.

'You're a very restless sleeper, *cara mia*,' Cesare censured softly, his breath fanning her cheek. 'I had to clamp you in one place to get peace.'

'Oh…' Lizzie framed dry-mouthed, entranced by her view of his lean, darkly handsome features in the golden dawn light, even her hearing beguiled by his melodic accent.

'Archie, on the other hand, sleeps like the dead and doesn't move at all,' Cesare quipped. 'I've never had a dog in my bed before.'

'There's a first time for everything.'

'First and *last*,' he stressed. 'Unfortunately you wouldn't settle without him last night.'

'I'm sorry I drank too much.' Colour slowly rose to drench her porcelain skin as he stared down at her. 'Was I really awful?'

Long fingers stroked her taut ribcage, making her violently aware of the breasts swelling mere inches above. 'No, you were bright and breezy until the alcohol took its toll.'

Her breathing pattern fractured as she felt her nipples pinch tight while a hot, achy sensation hollowed between her legs. 'I'm not used to drinking like that,' she muttered jaggedly.

His golden eyes smouldered down at her and a wicked grin slanted his shapely lips, ensuring that the rate of her heartbeat accelerated. 'Don't make a habit of it.'

'Of course, I won't,' she began with a frown, tightening every muscle in an urgent, almost panic-stricken attempt to smother the sexual responses trickling through her and awakening every skin cell.

Cesare, who planned everything in Machiavellian detail, had not planned to kiss Lizzie. Having decided not to touch her, he fully expected to abide by that prohibition because he virtually never gave way to impulses. Unhappily for him, the burning desire to pin Lizzie to the bed and have wild, sweaty sex with her had no rational base: it was driven by pure instinct. And when she shifted her hips below the shirt that had most definitely ridden up to ensure that bare skin met bare skin, Cesare was lost.

One minute, Lizzie was drowning in dark golden eyes framed by lashes longer than her own and downright jealous of the fact, and the next Cesare brought his mouth crashing down on hers with the kind of raw, driving passion that she was defenceless against. It was glorious and the taste of his tongue delving deep into the moist interior of her mouth was unsurpassable and an intoxication in its own right.

He traced the pointed bud of a straining nipple and her spine undulated of its own accord, sensation piercing straight to her pelvis. Her breasts had suddenly become achingly sensitive to the palms cupping them and the fingers tugging gently on the prominent tips. That felt amazingly good. A stifled gasp was wrenched from low in her throat and her spine arched, her body rising up to cradle his in an involuntary move of welcome as old as time. He skated his fingers along a slender thigh to discover the hot wet core of her, sliding between the delicate folds to moisturise the tiny bud of thrumming nerve endings above with a skilled fingertip.

Lizzie tore her lips from his to cry out,

hungry beyond bearing for that sensual touch and plunging her fingers into his tousled black hair to hold him to her. She was no more capable of thinking about what she was doing than she was of stopping breathing on command. Her heart was thumping, her ragged gasping breaths audible, her entire body was tingling madly with seething heat and need. With his free hand, he ripped at the buttons of the shirt. The shirt fell partially open, exposing the rounded fullness of a breast crowned by a pale pink nipple. He closed his mouth there, teasing the distended bud with the flick of his tongue and the graze of his teeth while his fingers stoked an erotic blaze at her feminine core. She shuddered, talon claws of fierce need biting into her, shock assailing her that anything physical could feel so intense that she could neither fight it nor control it.

'I love the way you respond to me, *mi piace*,' Cesare growled with satisfaction while switching his attention between her pouting breasts and sending fantastic ripples of ravishing sensation right down to her unbearably hot core.

Lizzie couldn't find her voice, her breath or a single functioning brain cell. Her entire being was welded to his every caress, wanting, needing more. And kissing an erotic path down over her flat, quivering stomach, Cesare gave her much more and she didn't have the strength of will to deny him.

With ruthless cool he zeroed in on the tender heart of her with every weapon in his erotic mastery, stroking delicate flesh with his tongue and his mouth and his expert fingers. Lizzie careened into shock at the intimacy and then moaned below the onslaught of wicked, delirious excitement. Intense pleasure followed, sweeping her up into a wild, yearning climb towards a peak that she felt she would never reach. But that climb was unstoppable. Suddenly her body wasn't her own any more and she was flying like a comet into the sun in a climax so powerful it brought shaken tears of reaction to her eyes.

Still ragingly aroused, Cesare sprang out of bed, his fists angrily clenched. What the hell had he been thinking of? No matter how great the temptation, he should *never* have touched her. They had a business agreement and a planned marriage of convenience ahead of them. They were not lovers, not friends with benefits. He did not want to muddy the waters with the kind of physical intimacy that women often assumed meant more than it did. If he wasn't careful, he might find himself more married than he had ever wanted to be, he acknowledged grimly.

Paralysed by a crazy sense of peace in the aftermath of orgasm, Lizzie closed her eyes, her body still trembling from the sweet aftermath of agonising pleasure. The mattress gave but she didn't open her eyes again until a phone rang, shattering her dream state. The phone fell silent in answer to a man's voice speaking Italian. Her lashes lifted then and she stared at Cesare while he paced the floor, mobile phone clamped to his ear. He still wore his boxers and his state of arousal was blindingly obvious. An almost painful tide of colour burned her face.

He tossed the phone down by the bed. 'Do you want the shower first?'

That prosaic question made Lizzie frantically pull the edges of the shirt she wore closed and she sat up in an agony of discomfiture. 'I'll go back to my own room.'

As she scrambled out of bed and reached for Archie, Cesare murmured without any expression at all, 'We made a mistake and we won't repeat it.'

Clutching Archie in an awkward hold,

Lizzie attempted to pick up her discarded clothing one-handed. 'Is that all you've got to say?' she prompted shakily.

'It was just sex…nothing worth fussing over,' Cesare opined in a tone that was as cold as a winter shower on her overheated skin. 'Look, I'll see you downstairs in an hour. I have some papers you have to sign before I leave.'

'You're going away again?' she asked in surprise, fighting the roar of temper rising from a secret place deep down inside her.

'We have forty-eight hours to go before the wedding and I intend to use it,' he advanced calmly, deep-set dark eyes hooded, wide, sensual mouth clenched hard.

Just sex…nothing worth fussing over? Lizzie mulled that putdown over while she showered. She wasn't hurt by his dismissal, of course she wasn't. *A mistake that would not be repeated.* Didn't she feel the same way as he did? What had happened shouldn't have happened. It was much more sensible if they stayed uninvolved and detached. So, if he had left her feeling a little crushed and foolish, it was her own fault for acting like an idiot and inviting such a denouement. If she couldn't quite shake off the sense of intimacy he had imbued her with, it was only because she had been more intimate with him than she had ever been with anyone else but that was a secret not for sharing...

CHAPTER FIVE

LIZZIE FASTENED THE cropped trousers and straightened the lilac cashmere sweater she wore with it. Her feet shod in flat ballerina pumps, her face lightly made up, she bore not the smallest resemblance to the woman she had been a mere week earlier.

Of course she was now in possession of a vast wardrobe and owned a choice of outfits for every conceivable occasion. Most probably many of the garments would never be worn because she could not imagine Cesare taking her sailing or out to dinner or indeed to the kind of dressy venue where she would require a full-length gown. The wardrobe was totally wasteful in its size and probable expense but she had already learned that once Cesare had instructed his underlings that she was to be dressed from head to toe in designer fashion, his orders were carried out without question.

A pity she was a little more rebellious in that line, Lizzie acknowledged wryly. A lifetime of counting the pennies meant that extravagance made her feel guilty. Breakfast in bed made her feel even guiltier although, to be honest, any excuse to escape the ghastly prospect of having to breakfast alone with Cesare had been extremely welcome.

After all, she had made a huge fool of herself the night before, hadn't she?

Lizzie inwardly cringed, colour marking her cheeks afresh. It would be a very long time, if ever, before she contrived to forget how she had writhed in ecstasy in Cesare's bed. But mercifully, they hadn't actually got as far as having full sex, she reminded herself bracingly, and she assumed that that reality would make it a little easier for her to reinstate normal boundaries between them. She was no natural wanton, never had been, had simply let alcohol, curiosity and temptation steer her briefly in the wrong direction. She wasn't like her mother either because she was not prone to sudden blinding infatuations. For years, there had been no other man for her but Andrew, a reality that had made the slow death of their relationship all the more painful to endure because it had started out with such high hopes.

It offended her sense of decency, however, that the intimacy she had shrunk from exploring with Andrew, whom she had loved, could be so very tempting when offered by a male like Cesare Sabatino, who had no respect for her at all. Cesare didn't give two hoots what happened to her or how she felt about any issue. Cesare merely wanted to *use* her to regain the island of Lionos and he thought that paying her richly for the privilege should take care of any doubts she might have.

'Mr Sabatino is in the office at the end of the corridor,' Primo informed her as she reached the foot of the grand staircase.

Almost sick with self-consciousness, Lizzie found the door ajar and walked in without knocking. Cesare's arrogant dark head flew up from his laptop, subdued fire flaring in his dark, glittering eyes at the interruption until he realised who his visitor was. A well-bred smile lightened his darkly handsome features and curved his hard mouth as he leapt upright, his attention automatically pinning to the lissom curves revealed by the casually elegant outfit she wore. In startling comparison a pink and white X-rated image of Lizzie splayed across his bed erupted at the back of Cesare's mind and he ground his teeth together as his body leapt in response to the provocation. Not for the first time he regretted the interruption that had left him burning with sexual frustration.

When he had last called Celine, he had grasped that he had a problem he had not foreseen. Aware that he was getting married, his French lover no longer wished to be seen in his company. Celine guarded her reputation because the clients who paid her a small fortune to advertise their exclusive perfume were conservative and Cesare had perfectly understood her determination to put her career first. It was, nonetheless, a challenge for him to work out how he was to cope for the next few months being married and *not* married at the same time.

He had not gone without sex for more than a couple of weeks since he was a teenager. Was he now supposed to sneak around seeking a discreet outlet? Without a doubt, he would have to avoid being seen consorting with any woman other than his wife or their marriage would appear dubious and, after going to such lengths to bring about the marriage, that was not a risk he was prepared to take. Whether he liked it or not and whether anything came of it or not, Lizzie was his only option for the foreseeable future, he acknowledged grudgingly.

'You look terrific, *cara*,' Cesare told Lizzie truthfully, politely tugging out a chair for her to use. The jasmine scent of her perfume flared his nostrils and before he could suppress the memory he recalled the wild, hot sweetness of her response. No man could easily forget that kind of passion, he reasoned, exasperated by his stubborn libido and the effect those turbulent hormones had on his usually cool intellect.

'Thanks but it's all fancy packaging, not really me,' Lizzie parried uncomfortably, because he was towering over her and close enough that she could smell the citrusy cologne that overlaid the erotic undertones of clean, warm male. Her colour fluctuating, she sat very straight-backed in her seat.

'Learn how to accept a compliment gracefully,' Cesare advised softly. 'You have a great figure, gorgeous hair and a beautiful face. Clothes merely provide an effective frame for the looks that nature gave you.'

Lizzie dealt him a pained half-smile. Unlike her, he was a master of the ready word and the right thing to say and had probably never been stuck for a quote in his entire gilded life. She evaded his shrewd gaze because she felt vulnerable, almost naked in his presence, stripped as she was of her usual working clothing and countryside assurance because his privileged world was so foreign to hers. She loved the way good clothes that fitted perfectly made her feel, but she wondered if he would still want her without that superficial gloss, a thought that made her feel inadequate and a little pathetic. In short, the spectacular luxury of his home, the costly garments and the preponderance of staff made Lizzie feel out of her depth and drowning. All she had required to crown her discomfiture was that ill-judged sexual episode that morning. 'I want you to sign these documents.' Evidently impervious to the unease afflicting Lizzie, Cesare extended a slim sheaf of papers. 'I need your permission to make alterations to the villa on Lionos.'

Her brow furrowed in surprise. 'Alterations? But you haven't even *seen* the house yet.'

'Because we won't be married until Friday,' Cesare pointed out drily. 'While we're on our honeymoon in Italy, my grandmother will be having her surgery and recuperating. As soon as she is strong enough we will fly out to Lionos and stay in the villa with her.'

'I didn't realise we were having a honeymoon.'

'It will only be a honeymoon in the eyes of the outside world,' Cesare qualified wryly.

'And your grandmother falls into that category too?' Lizzie checked.

'I've already explained that,' Cesare reminded her. 'For all that Athene's strong, she's an old lady. I don't want her to guess that our marriage is a fake. If she knew the truth she'd feel responsible and unhappy.'

'I can understand that.' Lizzie studied him uneasily. He emanated sleek, expensive elegance in a black business suit that outlined his broad shoulders, narrow hips and long, powerful legs to perfection but, unfortunately for Lizzie, she was still seeing him in his form-fitting boxers, an energising image of him half-naked and rampant with masculine potency. She chewed hard at the soft underside of her lower lip, fighting her awareness and her disobedient and thoroughly embarrassing thoughts.

'Before we can stay at the villa, however,

some improvements must be made to the accommodation and for that I require your permission as the property belongs to you and your sister.'

'What sort of improvements?' Lizzie prompted with a frown.

'I want to send Primo out to the island immediately with a team of kitchen and bathroom specialists. The house needs to be brought up to date before we can live there and I want to ensure that Athene enjoys her stay.'

'But won't she be sentimental about changes being made to the house where she grew up?' Lizzie asked in surprise.

'That's a fair point but times have changed since she was a girl and I believe she'll recognise that. She's a practical woman and she likes her comforts.'

'From what my mother said, most of the soft furnishings will need to be replaced as well,' Lizzie told him in wry warning. 'Drapes, beds, sofas. I don't think it's possible to achieve so much within such a short time frame and if you don't watch out...once you start removing fitments, the villa will quickly become uninhabitable.'

His supreme assurance untouched, Cesare

dealt her an amused smile. 'Believe me, if I'm prepared to throw enough money at the problem, someone will accept the challenge, *cara*.'

Lizzie shrugged because it was immaterial to her what he chose to have done to a house that she had never seen and would only briefly visit. But it was a painful reminder that Cesare only wanted her because she owned the island and could sell it to him if he married her and nobody, but nobody, could make a relationship out of that, she told herself wretchedly. None of her anxious feelings showing on her face, she dutifully scribbled her signature in the indicated places and provided her sister's address for the documents to be couriered to her.

A wholehearted smile softened her taut mouth when Archie poked his head round the door and trotted across the polished wooden floor to greet his mistress.

Cesare watched the dog receive a warm welcome and decided it was educational. Archie looked pathetic with only three working legs and the fourth in a cast and the dog played his advantage for all he was worth, rolling his tummy up in the air to be petted and then struggling pitifully to get up off the floor again. Cesare bent down to lift the terrier and help him upright again. In reaction to his sudden proximity, Lizzie rammed her chair back out of the way, her nervous response setting Cesare's teeth on edge as he straightened again.

Lizzie collided with stunning dark golden eyes fringed with black velvet lashes and forgot how to breathe, feverish tension snaking through her every muscle as she rose hurriedly from her chair again and moved towards the door, keen to be gone.

'Your father and your sister will be attending the wedding?' Cesare sought confirmation.

'Yes…' Lizzie coughed to clear her convulsed throat. 'And I'll ring Chrissie now to explain about the papers she has to sign.'

'I doubt if I'll see you again before we meet at the church on Friday,' Cesare imparted softly. 'Somehow try to practise not leaping away when I come close. It's a dead giveaway that our relationship is a sham.'

Lizzie flushed with mortification. 'Then practise keeping your distance,' she advised.

Well, that was telling him, Cesare conceded grimly. She was angry with him. He had been less than diplomatic after that phone call that interrupted them earlier that day. He ground his even white teeth together. He had only told the truth. Did women always punish men for telling the truth? If their arrangement was to work, however, he would need to make more of an effort to sustain their relationship, he acknowledged grudgingly. Women were emotional creatures. Her anxious, uneasy attitude towards him had just underlined that unwelcome reality.

Furthermore, Lizzie might be a gold-digger who had chosen money over ethics when given the choice, but how could he blame her for that when she had lived in poverty for so many years? It was not a crime for her to seek to better herself. And how could he fault her avaricious streak when, without it, she would have sent him and his proposition packing? It was unjust of him to view her in the same unforgiving light as the many mercenary women who had shared his bed, he conceded wryly. Serafina, after all, had made a straight-up choice to ditch Cesare and marry a man who had been much wealthier, even though he was also much older. He had to be less judgemental and more generous to Lizzie. In any case, as his wife and potentially the future mother of his child, Lizzie was also the equivalent of a long-term project. Somehow he would have to make her happy and *keep* her happy, because if he didn't all his plans could still come to nothing.

'You look totally amazing!' Chrissie exclaimed as Lizzie spun to show off her wedding gown, slender shoulders and arms sheathed in the finest see-through lace, her tiny waist accentuated by the fullness of her skirt.

'My brother's a closet romantic. He's going to love that dress,' Maurizia forecast as a knock sounded on the door and she and Sofia went to answer it.

'I'm having so much fun. I wish I hadn't put that exam ahead of attending your hen do,' Chrissie lamented, a slight willowy figure in the topaz-coloured bridesmaid dress that she and Cesare's sisters all wore.

Lizzie gazed fondly at her sister, thinking that she was the real beauty in the family with her perfect features and superior height.

'A pressie for you from Cesare,' Sofia announced, placing a jewel case in Lizzie's hands.

A gloriously delicate diamond necklace and drop earrings met Lizzie's stunned appraisal and a chorus of admiration rose from her companions. Of course, Cesare was playing to the gallery, assuming the role of besotted bridegroom for his siblings' benefit, Lizzie guessed. She put on the necklace and the earrings and realised that she was rather pathetically wishing that her wedding were the genuine article. She loved Cesare's family and would have given just about anything for them to be her family as well. Instead she had to live with the unlovely truth that she was deceiving them and would soon be deceiving Cesare's grandmother as well.

'You're really sure about doing this?' Chrissie whispered in the church porch as she made an unnecessary adjustment to Lizzie's gown while their father hovered, looking irritable. 'Because it's not too late to change your mind. All I have to do is call a taxi and we're out of here.'

'Are you trying to cause trouble? Of course, she's not going to change her mind!' Brian Whitaker declared in exasperation. 'That Sabatino fellow has to be the best thing that ever happened to her! At least he has an ounce of sense between his ears.'

'*We* certainly think so,' Paola piped up

without hesitation. 'But sometimes the bride does get cold feet.'

'Not this one,' Lizzie countered steadily, smoothing over the awkwardness that had settled over the bridal party with her father's tactless words.

Cesare turned to look at Lizzie only when she reached the altar. Eyes the colour of melted bronze assailed her and she stopped breathing, gripped by the ferocious force of will in that appraisal. He had no doubts, she interpreted. He knew exactly what he was doing, had come to terms with the drawbacks and was concentrating on the end game. She had to do the same, she told herself urgently. She had to stop trying to personalise their relationship and stop wondering whether or not he would kiss her after they had been pronounced man and wife. Such treacherous thoughts were far removed from business-like behaviour and utterly inappropriate, she scolded herself in exasperation.

'You look fantastic,' Cesare murmured softly while he threaded the wedding band onto her finger and she followed suit, copying his manoeuvre with less cool and more nerves.

Indeed, Cesare was taken aback by just

how fabulous she looked. The effect she had on him was ever so slightly unnerving. It was his libido, he told himself impatiently. As long as he stuck to his rules of never getting tangled in anything that smacked of an emotional connection, he would be fine and perfectly happy.

And then the deed was done and they were married and there was no kiss, nor indeed any instruction to kiss the bride. Her hand trembling on Cesare's arm, she walked down the aisle, seeing a sea of smiling faces on every side of her. It was not her idea of a small wedding because the big church was crammed with guests. Out on the steps, Cesare escorted a tiny woman with vibrant brown eyes set in a round wrinkled face to meet her.

'Athene…meet Elisabetta, known as Lizzie,' he murmured quietly. 'Lizzie, this is my grandmother.'

The two women stood chatting about nothing in particular for several minutes beneath Cesare's watchful eye. Athene grinned at Lizzie. There was an astonishing amount of mischief in that unexpected grin and she squeezed Lizzie's hand. 'We'll talk later,' she promised cheerfully.

Later became much later once the bridal

merry-go-round took over. The bride and groom greeted their guests at the country house hotel chosen to stage the reception, dined in splendour while being entertained by a famous singer, listened to the speeches and danced the first dance with Lizzie stumbling over her own feet. In the circle of Cesare's powerful arms and surrounded by so many well-wishers, Lizzie had to struggle to remember that their wedding was a fake.

In fact when Cesare lowered his darkly handsome head and kissed her, Lizzie was so unprepared for the move and so taken back by it she fell into it like a child falling down a bottomless well. His mouth moved on hers and his tongue darted across the roof of her mouth and excitement leapt so high inside her she felt dizzy and intoxicated, her head tilting back, her hands tightening round his neck, fingertips flirting with the silky strands of his black hair. It was heavenly and devastating; heavenly to glory in her womanhood and appreciate that she had now discovered her sensual side and devastating to register that the wrong man was punching her buttons, simply to impress their audience.

In passionate rejection of that belittling image, Lizzie jerked her head back and pressed him back from her. 'Enough...' she muttered unsteadily.

'*Dio mio,* not half enough for me, *bellezza mia,*' Cesare rasped in a driven undertone. 'I want you.'

Lizzie had become as stiff as a board. 'We talked about that and decided that it wasn't sensible.'

'To hell with being sensible!' Cesare shot back at her with smouldering dark golden eyes framed by black velvet lashes, so breathtakingly handsome in that moment that he took her breath away. 'Passion isn't sensible... don't you know that yet?'

No, but he was teaching her what she had never wanted to know. Experimentation was acceptable to Lizzie as long as she remained in control. She didn't want to be out of control, didn't want to risk getting hurt or making a fool of herself again. Suddenly all her worst fears were coalescing in the shape of Cesare Sabatino and she had only gone and married the guy!

Sofia approached her. 'Athene wants you to come and sit with her for a while. I expect she wants to get to know you... Cesare is by far her favourite grandchild.'

Lizzie rolled her eyes in sympathy. 'He's the only boy.'

'She practically raised him—that's why they're so close,' Sofia explained. 'Cesare was only four when our mother married his father and although he was supposed to come and live with our parents straight away, he and Athene kept on putting it off and Papa didn't like to interfere too much. Cesare's never been easy—he and Papa are so different.'

'Goffredo is a pet,' Lizzie said warmly. 'You're so lucky.'

'Cesare's too clever for his own good,' his sister opined. 'Papa was in awe of his brain and he was such an argumentative little boy.'

A smile of amusement tilted Lizzie's mouth. 'I can imagine. He likes everything his own way.'

Athene patted the comfortable armchair beside her own. 'Tell me about yourself. I'm a typical nosy old lady,' she confided. 'You talk and I ask the questions.'

Naturally there were questions about Lizzie's mother, whom Athene had met while Goffredo was dating her.

'My son could not have made her happy.' Cesare's grandmother sighed with regret. 'Francesca was always dissatisfied and she was disappointed that Goffredo already had a son. I wasn't that surprised when she broke off the engagement.'

'She wasn't happy with anyone for very long,' Lizzie admitted quietly.

'That must have been very difficult for you and your sister when you were growing up. The things that happen when you're young leave scars,' Athene remarked wryly. 'I believe that's why it's taken so long for Cesare to put Serafina behind him where she belongs…'

'Serafina?' Lizzie queried tentatively, wondering worriedly if this was some family story that she should have been acquainted with and if her ignorance would strike the older woman as suspicious.

'I didn't think he would've mentioned her to you,' Athene told her with a wry smile. 'Cesare hides his vulnerabilities very effectively.'

Lizzie resisted the temptation to admit that she hadn't believed he had any.

'Cesare fell in love with Serafina when he was a student. He wanted to marry her but she said she was too young,' Athene related, her wise old eyes resting on Lizzie's absorbed expression. 'In her first job, she met a very rich man in his seventies and within weeks they were wed.'

Lizzie froze in consternation. 'That must've been devastating for him,' she muttered ruefully, thinking that she had unkindly misjudged Cesare when she had assumed he simply had no heart and no room in his life for anything but business and profit.

'But today I know that he has finally put Serafina back where she belongs in the past,' his grandmother proclaimed with satisfaction and patted Lizzie's hand. 'Today I am joyful that Cesare has married you and changed the whole course of his life for the better.'

Lizzie suppressed a groan of disagreement. She was discovering where Goffredo's optimistic outlook came from—he had inherited it from his mother. It was a source of wonder to her that Cesare had grown up surrounded by people with such sunny natures and yet contrived to retain his cold, unemotional attitude to life. Yet he was also careful to maintain a certain distance from his loving family, she conceded reflectively, wondering if he secretly feared that his family loving softness might dull his own ruthless cutting edge.

A couple of hours after that, Lizzie boarded Cesare's private jet. Her feet, shod in spindly high heels, were killing her. Even the short walk through the airport had been too much and she collapsed into her leather upholstered seat and kicked off her shoes with intense relief.

'You did very well today,' Cesare pronounced, disconcerting her as he took his own seat opposite. 'I don't think anyone suspected the truth.'

'Your father knows,' she reminded him uncomfortably.

'He'll believe the truth for all of ten minutes. Give him a few weeks and he'll persuade himself that we fell madly in love within hours of getting married,' Cesare forecast with sardonic bite. 'That's the way Goffredo functions.'

'You have a lovely family,' Lizzie countered, colour springing into her cheeks. 'Don't be so critical. They love you very much and they aren't afraid to show it.'

Cesare stiffened until he recalled his father-in-law's behaviour throughout the day. Brian Whitaker had turned down the opportunity to make a speech, had kept to his own company in the midst of the crowd and had steadfastly managed not to smile even for the photographs. 'Your father's…different,' he conceded quietly. 'Not the demonstrative type.'

'When my mother left him, it soured him on life,' she muttered ruefully. 'And life has been tough for him ever since. He'll be more content living in the house he's hoping to rent in the village. I think it will be a relief for him not to be looking out of windows at the farm and fretting about the jobs I'm not getting done.'

'Isn't it a relief for you as well?' Cesare prompted, thinking of the long and gruelling hours of work she must have endured while she endeavoured to keep the farm going without help.

Lizzie compressed her lips and frowned reflectively. 'From dawn to dusk I worried about everything and anything and I'm not sorry to be free of that stress. The bank threatening to withdraw the loan was our biggest fear but then the rent was raised…and, that was a body blow, totally the last straw,' she confided honestly. 'That was followed by Chrissie announcing that she was going to drop out of uni and come home because we were having such a struggle. I couldn't let that happen. She *needed* to get her education.'

Cesare was listening intently. 'So that's

why you suddenly changed your mind and agreed to marry me?' he breathed in a tone of disconcertion. 'I had no idea that you were under that much financial and emotional pressure.'

'But you said you *knew* our situation,' she reminded him in surprise. 'I assumed you'd used a private investigator to check us out before you came to visit.'

Level dark eyes gazed back at her, a frown line pleating his ebony brows. 'No, I didn't. I didn't know about the bank loan, the rent rise or your sister's plans to drop out. I only knew about your father's ill health and that you were trying to keep the farm afloat on your own.'

'Well, you know the whole story now,' Lizzie commented mildly. 'I was ready to sell my soul for thirty pieces of silver.'

'*No,*' Cesare contradicted, his sibilant Italian accent vibrating in the silence to send a current of awareness travelling down her slender spine. 'You were desperate to protect your family, regardless of what it might cost you personally. That's loyalty and I admire that trait.'

As the silence stretched, Cesare went back to work at his laptop. Driven by something stronger than he was, he found himself glancing up to watch Lizzie leaf through a glossy fashion magazine, pulling faces whenever she came on a picture of any garment she considered too extreme while absently fondling Archie's ear beneath his balloon collar. She was so very natural. What you saw was what you got from Lizzie Whitaker and he had totally misunderstood her. It was a sobering discovery for a male who prided himself on his ability to read others. He had made all too many assumptions about Lizzie, not least that she was a gold-digger, and now that he had discovered that she had been driven more by desperation than greed his innate curiosity about her was finally set free.

'Why did you dye your hair brown?' he asked her abruptly.

Lizzie twined a shining silver strand round a self-conscious finger and winced in evident embarrassment. 'Andrew didn't like my hair. He thought it attracted too much attention and that it looked white and made people think I was an old lady at first glance,' she told him uncomfortably. 'I could see his point.'

'Did you really want to please him that much?' Cesare pressed. 'Your hair's beautiful, unusual but undeniably beautiful, *cara*.'

Lizzie shrugged but her face glowed at the compliment. His lean, darkly handsome features held her intent gaze and she switched her attention back to the magazine, a pool of liquid heat gathering in her pelvis that made her squirm with chagrin. He was so very, *very* good-looking, it was natural for her to stare a little, she told herself ruefully, but she had to keep her feet on the ground and learn to distinguish between what was real and what was more probably fake.

The limousine that collected them from the airport in Italy wended its way along winding roads and through some spectacular scenery. It was late spring and the fields were green with fava beans and wheat dotted with yellow broom. Medieval villages in picturesque hill-top locations were ringed by vineyards and olive groves while the rolling hills were covered with groves of cypresses and umbrella pines. Lizzie was enchanted and plied Cesare with questions.

'You still haven't told me where we're going,' she complained.

'We're almost there.'

Lizzie stared out at the rustic stone farmhouse on the ridge of the hill and blinked because it was not what she expected. Cesare was so sophisticated that she had been convinced that they were heading for some exclusive spa. 'It just doesn't look like your style,' she breathed helplessly.

'I love old buildings. When I first saw it I was a student out hiking with friends. The roof had fallen in, the first floor had gone and the end wall had collapsed. We took shelter in the barn during a thunderstorm,' Cesare explained as the driver turned down a dirt track that steadily climbed the hill. 'I watched the sun go down over the valley and swore I'd buy it with my first million.'

'Your first...*million*?' she exclaimed.

'It was a money pit,' Cesare told her cheerfully, his dark eyes gleaming with rueful amusement. 'I learnt that the hard way.'

The car drew up in a paved courtyard ornamented with urns full of tumbling flowers. As they climbed out, a rotund little woman in an apron hurried out to greet them. Her name was Maria and she was the housekeeper and, seemingly, Cesare's biggest fan. Ushered into a great vaulted hall, Lizzie looked around herself with keen interest, glancing through to a gracious drawing room rejoicing in a vast pale stone fireplace and an array of vibrant turquoise sofas. The outside might be antique and rustic but the inside was all contemporary elegance.

Maria led her upstairs and into a glorious light-filled bedroom with a window overlooking the valley below. Lizzie fingered the fine white linen bedding and admired the beautifully draped bed while wondering where Cesare was planning to sleep. The driver brought their cases up, closely followed by Cesare, lean and lithe in khaki chinos and an open-necked shirt that screamed Italian designer style.

'Where's your room?' Lizzie asked quietly.

'We *share*,' Cesare told her without skipping a beat.

'I'm not sharing a bed with you!' Lizzie gasped in consternation.

'We're supposed to be married. Let's stay in role,' Cesare fielded. 'Having gone this far, it would be stupid to take risks by using separate bedrooms.'

Lizzie kicked off her shoes and mulled over that argument. 'Maria's not going to talk.'

'She's not the only member of staff with access to the upper floor,' he shot back drily.

'OK…' Lizzie stood at the foot of the bed, prepared to admit that it was huge, but she was still doubtful that she could lose him in it. 'But you have to stay on *your* side of the bed.'

'Are we five years old now?' Cesare quipped, studying her with incredulity. 'You're making a fuss about nothing.'

Lizzie settled glinting witch-green eyes on him. 'I'm not used to sharing a bed. It's not nothing to me.'

'We'll discuss it over dinner,' Cesare decreed.

Lizzie threw her arms wide in emphasis, her temper mounting. 'I don't want to discuss it...I just don't want to do it!'

'Only forty-eight hours ago, you *did*,' Cesare countered, lean, strong face hard, dark golden eyes smouldering with recollection and unforgotten hunger.

Lizzie reddened. 'I was wondering how long it would take you to throw that back in my face. I was drunk, for goodness' sake,' she protested.

'At least you know what you want when you're drunk,' he riposted.

Lizzie slammed shut the door lest they be overheard arguing. 'That's a horrible thing to say!'

'Whether you like it or not, it's the truth.

You want me every bit as much as I want you. You just won't admit it.'

Lizzie was so enraged by that arrogant statement that she walked into the bathroom and closed the door behind her to escape him. The fixtures took her breath away. An antique tub took up prime position by the window while rustic stone walls and a pale marble floor provided an effective frame.

'And hiding in the bathroom isn't going to persuade me otherwise!' Cesare completed loudly outside the door.

Lizzie threw open the door again and marched out with compressed lips to drag one of the cases across the beautiful oak floor. 'I was *not* hiding.'

Cesare snatched up the case and planted it on the bed, helpfully springing the locks for her.

Lizzie hovered, her colour high, her eyes veiled.

Cesare stalked closer like a predator about to spring and she tensed from head to toe. 'Look at me, *bellezza mia*,' he urged.

Almost involuntarily, Lizzie lifted her head, platinum hair flying back from her heart-shaped face. 'Why?' she said flatly.

Lean brown hands lifted to frame her

cheekbones and turn her face up. A muscle pulled taut at the corner of his wide, sensual mouth. 'I want to make a baby with you the normal way. I don't want to use artificial insemination. If we're going to become parents, let's try the natural approach first.'

He had taken her entirely by surprise. Her entire face flamed and even worse the heat darted downward to engulf her whole body. 'But that's not what we agreed.'

'We didn't agree anything. You made a suggestion. I didn't like it but I wasn't prepared to argue about it at that point and turn you off the whole idea of marrying me,' Cesare admitted without hesitation.

His sheer honesty bemused her and then touched her deep. *I want to make a baby with you*. The very words made Lizzie melt and she tried to squash her reaction and deny it. It would not be safe or sensible to have actual sex with Cesare Sabatino because it would smash the barriers she had carefully erected. But the prospect of undergoing some cold scientific procedure in a fertility clinic was, she suddenly appreciated, even less attractive to her.

'I'll think about it,' Lizzie mumbled half under her breath. 'Now, if you don't mind,

I'd like to get changed into something more comfortable.'

'I'll go for a shower,' Cesare told her, peeling off his shirt without an ounce of inhibition.

Her heart hammering, Lizzie averted her gaze but the enthralling image of his bronzed, muscular torso was still seared across her vision. She pulled an outfit out of the case, nothing fancy for she had had her fill of fancy outfits that day. She caught an accidental glimpse of Cesare striding naked as the day he was born into the en suite and she almost groaned out loud. They were so different, so ill matched. He had seen it all, done it all, while she had only dreamt of the seeing and the doing. If she slept with him, she would develop feelings for him and she would get hurt because he wouldn't respond. Or maybe she would discover that she was the kind of woman who could have sex without getting more deeply involved, she reasoned abstractedly. She might not get attached to him at all, might be grateful to wave goodbye to him after a few months. How could she know how she would react?

When the shower was free, she made use of it and removed most of the heavy make-up she had worn for her big day. Applying only a dash of lipstick and blusher, she pulled on a stretchy maxi skirt and a sleeveless silk top, thrusting her feet into flat sandals. When she reappeared, a maid was in the bedroom hanging their clothes in the built-in closet and Lizzie went straight downstairs.

Cesare strode out to the marble-floored hall. 'Let me show you around before dinner,' he suggested.

'Where's Archie?' she asked.

Cesare held a finger to his handsome mouth in silencing mode and pointed into the drawing room. Archie was stretched out on a shaggy rug, his contented snores audible.

As dusk was folding in fast, Cesare showed her the outside of the house first. Lizzie stood on the covered stone terrace where Maria was fussing over a table covered in a snowy white cloth and admired the stunning view of the valley, which was overlooked by a superlative infinity pool. 'The views are out of this world. I'm not surprised you fell for this place,' she admitted, the tension of the day slowly seeping out of her.

Without warning, Cesare reached for her hand. 'This marriage can be as real as we want it to be, *bellezza mia*,' he pointed out quietly.

Her fingers flexed within the firm hold of his and her colour heightened. Real didn't mean for ever, did it? But then how many marriages truly lasted for ever? They were together now and would stay together until a child was born. The child she longed for, she reminded herself ruefully. Surely the closer she and Cesare became, the easier it would be to share their child both now and in the future?

Her lips parted almost without her volition, green eyes wide and anxious as if she was stunned by her own daring. 'I'll give it a go,' she told him softly. 'But I can't make any promises.'

Cesare smiled. It was a brilliant smile that illuminated his darkly beautiful features and enhanced his stubborn, passionate mouth. 'I'll try to make sure you don't regret it, *cara*.'

CHAPTER SIX

'MARIA IS WHIPPING out her entire repertoire for this one meal,' Cesare commented in amusement as the lazy meal wound through course after necessarily dainty course of appetising dishes.

Already unable to credit that she had agreed to try being married for *real*, Lizzie was too stressed to eat much of anything. A bite here and there was the best she could do and she proffered fervent apologies to the plump little cook when she came out to the terrace bearing her *pièce de résistance*, a fabulous layered chocolate cake.

They were about to embark on their marriage as if they were a normal married couple. And this was their *wedding night*. All of a sudden something Lizzie hadn't even had to consider in the run-up to the wedding was looming like a concealed tripwire in front of her. If she admitted that she was still a virgin he was sure to think she was a freak. After all, he knew she had been engaged. It would be better to keep quiet, she decided, and hope he didn't notice that there was anything different about her.

'You've barely touched alcohol today,' Cesare commented, wondering why she had fallen so quiet. Not that she was ever a chatterbox, he acknowledged wryly. In fact there was always a stillness about her, a sense of tranquillity at the heart of her that was disconcertingly attractive.

'In the light of our…er…plans,' Lizzie muttered awkwardly, 'I thought it was better to abstain.'

'You're referring to the alcohol and pregnancy safety debate?'

Kill me now, Lizzie thought melodramatically. 'Yes. The argument about what might be a safe level goes back and forth, so it seems wiser just to avoid it altogether.'

'Is that why you made the most of your hen night?' Cesare asked, strong jawline tensing as he remembered her on the dance floor, full of vital energy and playfulness as she cast off her usual restraint.

'No. That wasn't planned. I missed Chrissie,' she admitted, colouring, 'and it had just been a very long time since I had been out like that and I overindulged.'

'Don't beat yourself up about it,' Cesare urged, stunning dark golden eyes shimmering in the candlelight against his bronzed skin.

He was so…hot, he was literally on fire, Lizzie reflected dizzily. And she was married to him, about to share a bed with him… and she was fretting, shrinking, *sighing* over the fact? What was wrong with her? That chemistry he had mentioned was in overdrive, lighting her up from the inside out with a prickling, tingling energy that her body could no longer contain. In an abrupt movement, she rose from the table and walked to the edge of the terrace to study the lights of the fortified village on the other side of the valley.

Her heart was as locked up tight as that village, hidden behind high defensive walls, she reminded herself bracingly. Having sex with Cesare didn't mean she was about to get silly ideas about him and start pining when he was no longer available. She had watched her mother careen blindly from one man to the next, hooked on love, her drug of choice. Lizzie had loved once and learned her lesson. If she couldn't even make it work with

Andrew, there was little chance of it working with anyone else. She would have a baby to love though, she told herself in consolation.

'You're very tense, *cara*.' Cesare sighed, stilling behind her and gently resting his hands on her taut shoulders. Her delicate frame was dwarfed by his. 'You don't have to do anything you don't want to do…'

That he could read her nervous tension that accurately mortified Lizzie. In truth the problem was that she wanted him too much and feared the strength of that yearning. He turned her slowly round into the circle of his arms and she looked up at him and her knees went weak and her heart leapt in helpless response.

'I know that,' she asserted valiantly, wondering why he found the sudden change in their relationship so much easier. Were men just built that way? Was he more adaptable than she was? Or more relaxed at the concept of a marriage in which the only glue keeping them together would be sex and the hope of parenthood? *Just sex, nothing worth fussing over*, he had said after he got out of a bed where he had literally rocked her world. It was true that the only pleasure had been hers but his cold-blooded, practical take on what had happened between them had still knocked her for six. Yet she still couldn't drag her gaze from his beautifully shaped, passionate mouth.

Cesare studied her with veiled eyes, black lashes rimming the glint of smouldering gold. Desire was lancing through him with lightning-force potency, sending tiny ripples of tension through his big, powerful frame. He couldn't take his eyes off her lush mouth and the pouting crowns of her small breasts, which stirred softly below the fine silk of her top every time she shifted position.

It was years since Cesare had been so aware of a woman and he loathed the edgy bite of frustrated hunger that made him tense. He wanted to have sex with her and persuade his libido and his brain that, after all, she was just like any other woman he had bedded. He hadn't been with anyone since the day he had first met her and that bothered him. He hadn't wanted Celine when he'd had the opportunity and no other woman had since attracted his attention. Of course the problem was doubtless that his affair with Celine had run its natural course and left him bored. Lizzie was new and different, which had obvious appeal. There was even something strangely, weirdly sexy about the idea of getting her pregnant. He wasn't sure what it was but he knew that just the thought of it made him hard and ready. Given even the smallest encouragement, he would've ditched Maria's wedding banquet of a meal and headed straight for the bedroom.

Shaking off that foolish thought, Cesare gazed down at his bride with the sudden piquant recognition that she was his wife. *His* legal wife, *his* to have and to hold, *his* to protect. Without further ado, he pulled her close and kissed her, a husky growl sounding in the back of his throat when her firm little breasts brushed against his chest. She liked being carried; he remembered that and smiled. He hoisted her up into his arms and Archie scrambled up from his position of repose by the sun-warmed wall and barked in consternation at the sight of them.

'Keep quiet, Archie,' Cesare groaned. 'You can't come between a man and his wife…and I warn you, Lizzie, he's not sleeping with us tonight or any other night.'

Lizzie was challenged enough to think of sleeping with Cesare and her mouth was still tingling from the hungry pressure of his mouth. As he carried her upstairs she decided that she was turning into a shameless hussy. A gasp escaped her lips when she saw the bedroom, which had been transformed into a bower of candlelight and flowers while they had been dining. Candles flickered light from metal lanterns set round the room and lush vases of pristine white flowers completed the magical effect.

'Did you organise this?' Lizzie asked in wonderment when he settled her down at the foot of the bed.

Cesare laughed. 'No. Maria has waited a long time for me to find a wife and I think she's celebrating.'

Sudden shyness reclaimed Lizzie as he gazed down at her, the lights picking out the hollows below his high cheekbones, lending him an enigmatic quality. In that lambent light, he was truly beautiful, sleek and dark, exotic and compellingly male. With sure hands he pushed her hair back from her face, letting the long, silky strands flow down her back. He tipped up her face and claimed another kiss, feeding from the sweetness of her mouth with hungry fervour, crushing her soft full lips below his while her fingers clung to his shoulders.

'I've been thinking about this from the first

moment I saw you,' Cesare growled against her reddened mouth, his dark deep voice vibrating down her spinal cord, the very essence of masculinity.

'You do talk nonsense sometimes and please don't tell me that's a compliment that I should gratefully receive. The first time you saw me I was in my dungarees and looked a complete mess!' Lizzie protested on the back of a rueful laugh.

'There's no accounting for taste or the male libido,' Cesare quipped, impervious to her disagreement. 'I saw your face, your skin, your eyes…it was enough, *delizia mia*.'

'I like it when you talk Italian,' Lizzie confided breathlessly. 'You could be reciting the multiplication tables but it wouldn't matter. It's your accent, your voice, the pitch you use.'

Surprised by that unexpected burst of loquaciousness, Cesare grinned, a slanting wicked grin that utterly transformed his lean, darkly handsome face, wiping away the cool vigilance and control that was usually etched there. 'What I like most about you is that you surprise me all the time.'

'Right now I'm surprising me,' Lizzie told him truthfully, uncertainty darkening her hazel eyes as it crossed her mind that she was behaving impulsively, not something she made a habit of after growing up with an impetuous mother. But then she was *not* her mother, she reminded herself squarely, and at the age of twenty-four was surely old enough to make her own decisions.

He took her mouth in a long, intoxicating kiss and sober thought became too much of a challenge. A tension of a very different kind began to lace her body. She became ridiculously conscious of the silk rubbing against her swollen nipples and the dampness at her feminine core. Her body was responding to the chemistry between her and Cesare with a life of its own, blossoming like a flower suddenly brought into bloom by the sunshine. Only chemistry, *just* sex, she reflected in an abbreviated fashion as she warded off her insecurities. There was nothing to fear, nothing to be ashamed of, nothing she need avoid to protect herself. Dimly she was registering at some level of her brain that her mother's disastrous affairs had made her far too reluctant to take a risk on a man.

Her silk top fell in a colourful splash of silk to the wooden floor and, with a ragged sigh of appreciation, Cesare closed his hands to the pert swell of her breasts, his thumbs expertly capturing and massaging the protruding pink peaks until they were taut and throbbing and the very breath was catching in her tightening throat. Her hips dug into the mattress beneath her, seeking to sate the hollow ache tugging at her pelvis.

One-handed, he wrenched at his shirt. 'You see how I forget what I'm doing when I'm with you, *delizia mia*?' he rasped.

Lizzie only needed that invitation and she tugged at his shirt, delicate fingers stroking over his taut, muscular shoulders, adoring the heat and strength of him. He put his mouth to her neck and skimmed the tip of his tongue along her delicate collarbone and then, gently lowering her flat on the bed, he roamed down over her ribcage, sending delicious little jolts of desire through her each time he captured the tender peaks of her breasts.

Passion had claimed Lizzie. Her temperature was rocketing higher and higher, a sheen of perspiration on her brow, and her heart was hammering so fast it felt as if it were at the foot of her throat. Her hand delving into his luxuriant black hair, she pulled him up to her and kissed him with all the urgent hunger racing through her. He pushed her skirt up above her knees and trailed his fingers slowly up her inner thighs. Every inch of her felt stretched taut with the extreme wanting that had taken her over and she gritted her teeth as he anchored his fingers to her knickers and trailed them off. She wanted his touch so bad it hurt and she squirmed in a fever of need.

'I'm trying to go slow,' Cesare bit out raggedly, 'but I feel like an express train.'

'Talking too much,' she told him, her teeth chattering together at the unwelcome pause.

With an almighty effort, Cesare stepped back from the source of temptation. Haste wasn't cool, especially not the first time. He didn't think a woman had ever responded with that much passion to him and it was setting him on fire with overriding need. He told her that in Italian and she gave him a blissful smile, evidently glorying in the sound of his language or his voice or whatever it was that she liked. He stripped off the shirt, unzipped his chinos, pushed off everything in one urgent forceful assault on his clothing. Naked, he came back to her, revelling in the way her eyes locked to him and the sudden blush that warmed her porcelain complexion. He couldn't recall when he had last been with a woman who blushed. And in the bedroom? Never.

Lizzie was transfixed. There he was in all his glory, her every piece of curiosity answered in one fell swoop. He scooped her up in his arms, pulled off the skirt that was her only remaining garment and settled her down, equally naked, in the centre of the turned-back bed.

Lizzie froze. 'I think we need to put out the candles!' she exclaimed, her entire body burning with embarrassment as she grasped in desperation for the sheet, which was out of reach.

In the very act of surveying her pale slender curves with rapt attention Cesare raised stunning golden eyes to study her in growing wonderment. 'I've already seen you naked,' he reminded her gently.

'That's different...I was too hung-over to be shy!' Lizzie pointed out loudly.

Cesare grinned and with a stretch of a long brown arm flipped up the sheet. 'This is not likely to hold me back,' he warned her.

As the cool cotton settled over her quivering length Lizzie lost some of her tension. Resting on one arm, she found Cesare gazing down at her with slumberous dark golden eyes. He rubbed a slightly stubbled jaw against her cheek in a sensual gesture on his path to her ready mouth.

One kiss melted into the next but as his hands roved skilfully over her, lingering on pulse points and teasing erogenous zones, lying still beneath his ministrations became tougher and tougher. Her nipples throbbed from his attentions, sending arrows of fire down to the tender, pulsing heart of her.

He stroked her and her spine arched. 'You're so wet, so ready for me,' Cesare husked.

A tiny shiver racked her slight frame, all the heat coalescing in the swollen, delicate tissue between her thighs. She squeezed her eyes tight shut, striving to stay in control and not betray how new it all was to her. But with every ravishing caress, he seduced her away from control. Soft gasps parted her lips, her neck extending, tendons clenching as the stimulation became almost too much to bear.

'You know this will be a first for me, *cara*,' Cesare confided, running the tip of his tongue across a turgid rose-pink nipple.

Lizzie could hardly find her voice. 'What will?'

'Sex without a condom…I've never done that before and it excites me,' he admitted huskily, shifting against her thigh, letting her feel the smooth, hard length of his erection.

Lizzie was trying not to think about the size of him in that department. She was a modern woman, well acquainted with averages and gossip and popular report. Being a virgin didn't mean she was entirely ignorant, she told herself in consolation, striving not to stress as her excitement built and built. Hands biting into his strong shoulders, she lifted her hips upward, succumbing to an almost uncontrollable urge to get closer to him. He toyed with her lush, damp opening, honeyed quivers of sensations rippling through her womb, and circled the tiny bud of her arousal until almost without warning a wild, seething force of irresistible sensation engulfed her like a flood. Her eyes flew wide and she bucked and jerked and sobbed in the grip of rush after rush of intense and enthralling pleasure.

He tipped her up, hooking her legs over his shoulders in a move that unnerved her. He plunged into her tight channel and for a moment she was preoccupied with the sense of fullness, the certain knowledge that this was exactly what her body had craved throughout his teasing foreplay. In fact everything was wonderful until the hot glide of his flesh within hers sank deeper and a sudden sharp, tearing pain made her stiffen and cry out in dismay.

Cesare froze as though a fire alarm had gone off and stared down at her, dark golden eyes like hungry golden flames in his lean bronzed face. 'You *can't* be...'

Enraged by her own bodily weakness and chagrin, Lizzie dealt him a look that would have dropped a grizzly bear at ten paces. 'Well, don't stop now.'

'You're a *virgin*?' Cesare emphasised, his incredulity unconcealed as he held himself at an angle above her, muscles straining in his bulging forearms.

'How's that your business?' Lizzie slung back argumentatively.

Cesare swore long and low in his own language and cursed her stubbornness. He burned for her but he was fighting his hunger with all his might. It struck him as unjust that the hot, tight hold of her body on his gave him pure pleasure while she had only experienced pure pain.

'It's my business,' he told her grimly. 'I think this is my cue to back off.'

'No... No!' Lizzie exclaimed in consternation. 'You don't get to go that far and then *stop*… I want to know what it's like…'

In receipt of that plaintive plea, Cesare groaned out loud, belatedly recognising that marriage was proving a much bigger challenge than he had expected. She was experimenting with him, he thought in all-male horror.

'Please…' Lizzie added, tugging him down to her, pale fingers framing his cheekbones as she reached without success for his beautiful, passionate mouth.

In the mood to be easily encouraged, Cesare shifted his hips, his entire attention nailed to her flushed and expressive face so that he could register the smallest wince she might make. Instead Lizzie smiled up at him with a look of wonderment that was uniquely soothing to his momentarily threatened male ego.

Lizzie closed her eyes again, mortified at the fuss she had made, the lengths she had had to go to to persuade him to continue. She had always believed that a man found it hard to stop in the middle of sex, so the fact that he had offered to withdraw altogether did not strike her as a compliment. But she had wanted to know, had wanted so badly to know what all the fuss was about.

He moved against her and tingling, driving sensation awakened in her pelvis again. She relaxed a little. The slow, almost provocative thrusts became enticing and she relaxed completely, indeed began to arch up to greet him with an enthusiasm she had never expected to feel. His skilled acceleration delivered sensation like nothing she had ever experienced and her excitement soared to delirious heights that climbed and climbed until she reached a peak and soared effortlessly over it and then down and down into the cocoon of lethargy and satiation, exhaustion pulling at her every sense.

Cesare settled her back down on the pillows and smoothed her tangled hair off her damp brow. His hand trembled a little because he was struggling to do two opposing things: firstly treat Lizzie like the bride she was and, secondly, suppress the anger tearing at him. 'Why didn't you tell me I'd be your first lover?' he demanded in a roughened undertone.

His tone, his exasperation, cut through Lizzie in her sensitive state like the sudden painful slice of a knife and she sat up abruptly, clutching the sheet to her chest. 'I didn't see that it was anything to do with you.'

'In other words, you chose to deliberately conceal it,' he condemned, leaping out of bed in one lithe, powerful movement. 'How the hell could you still be a virgin when you were once engaged?'

'Don't you dare raise your voice to me, Cesare Sabatino!' Lizzie yelled back at him furiously, but she was trembling with an innate fear she could not have expressed at that moment. 'As for why I was still a virgin, that's private.'

'You're married to me now, *cara*. I don't think it's unreasonable of me to expect an answer to something so basic.'

'When you have the right to ask me private questions, I'll let you know,' Lizzie slung back flatly, snaking out of the far side of the bed to avoid him and yanking the sheet free of the mattress with a violent jerk to wrap it round her body. 'Now, I'm going for a bath.'

'*Lizzie…*' Cesare ground out in frustration to her rigid back as she reached for the door of the en suite.

'I'm not feeling nice, *wifely* or the slightest bit chatty right now, so please excuse me,' Lizzie breathed icily and stepped into the bathroom, shutting and locking the door behind her within seconds.

Lizzie filled the glorious antique bath to the brim, filled it with bubbles and lowered her body into the warm water. Angry, Cesare could be incredibly intimidating, towering over her, dark eyes glowing with hostility in his lean dark face. She couldn't help that her first reaction to an angry man was to run to the nearest place of safety. Her mother's violent second husband had taught her to get herself and Chrissie out of harm's way fast.

But Lizzie refused to *be* intimidated by Cesare, whom she sensed would never be violent. What did he have to be so angry about? Hadn't their lovemaking been good for him? It had certainly been good for her, apart from the hiccup as such in the middle when she had discovered that her first experience of intimacy could actually be painful. Ironically she was more hurt by Cesare's withdrawal and grim mood in the aftermath, which had made her feel—all over again—inadequate. Why couldn't he have simply let the subject go? Had he no sensitivity? Couldn't he see that she didn't want to talk about it?

Cesare paced the bedroom in fierce frustration. Why hadn't she warned him? Had she been embarrassed about being untouched? He recalled the blushing and gritted his teeth, acknowledging that he was totally unfit to deal with sexual innocence when he had failed to recognise it even though it was right there in front of him. He had screwed up, screwed up even worse when he sprang an immediate interrogation on her.

This was not how he had pictured their marriage kicking off. She was all emotional now, very probably weeping in the bath and regretting their new agreement while wishing she had never laid eyes on him. And yet the sex had been amazing…so amazing he couldn't wait to repeat it. Galvanised into motion by that shameless motivation, Cesare threw on a disreputable pair of jeans and padded downstairs, pondering possibilities to redeem himself in his offended bride's eyes. Before he even got that far he heard the distant howls of Archie marooned in an outside kennel and he grinned at the sound. He was a very clever man and he would turn the wedding-night breakdown back into a honeymoon regardless of what sacrifices it demanded of him!

Archie broke off his cries mid-howl and

pranced towards him on three little legs. Archie was not particularly attached to Cesare but he recognised him as a potential lead to his mistress...

CHAPTER SEVEN

ARCHIE WHIMPERED OUTSIDE the bathroom door.

'You know you can do better than that,' Cesare told him, tossing him a fragment of chicken from one of the plates on the table by the bed.

For a three-legged dog, Archie could move fast and he caught the scrap in mid-air.

'Now...you have a mission,' Cesare reminded the scruffy little animal. 'You get her out of the bathroom.'

Archie hovered by the door, tried to push it but the balloon collar round his neck got in the way. Sitting back on his haunches, Archie loosed a sad howl that would not have shamed a banshee. Cesare threw him another piece of succulent chicken in reward. Archie gave a grand performance.

Lizzie woke up feeling cold, water sloshing noisily around her as she sat up wide-eyed.

Archie was howling at the door…or had that just been a dream? Clambering hastily out of the bath, she snatched up a fleecy towel and wrapped herself in it, just as Archie howled again. Glancing at the watch on the vanity to see how long she had slept, she was taken aback to realise that a couple of hours had passed and that it was now almost one in the morning. Depressing the lock, she opened the door in haste.

'Oh, pet, I forgot about you! Have you been lonely?' Lizzie asked, squatting down to the little dog's level.

'Want some supper?' Cesare asked lazily from the bed on which he reclined.

Small bosom swelling at that insouciant tone, Lizzie was about to tell him in no short order what he could do with supper and then her tummy growled and she registered in surprise that she was actually very hungry. Of course, she hadn't eaten very much at dinner…

Straightening, she looped her damp hair back behind her ear and focused on Cesare's lean, darkly devastating face, clashing with the banked-down glitter of his stunning eyes. 'You still want answers, don't you?'

'I'd be a liar if I said otherwise,' he admitted, sprawling back with his hands linked behind his head, a position which only threw into prominence the muscular torso and flat ribbed stomach beneath his black T-shirt.

Lizzie breathed in slowly, belatedly registering the table of snacks by the bed and the candles that must have been relit while she slept. A surprising sense of calm after the storm enclosed her. The worst had already happened, hadn't it? What did she have to fear now? Not marriage, not sex, she decided, her chin coming up. Cesare had...*briefly*... scared her but that wasn't his fault. No, that fault could be laid at the door of her late mother's misjudgement of men and a stepfather who had given Lizzie nightmares long after he had passed out of her life.

'You know, when you got so angry, you scared me,' she told him baldly. 'My mother was married to a man who beat her up when he got angry.'

Cesare sprang off the bed, a frown pleating his ebony brows. 'I would never hurt you.'

'I think I know that already,' Lizzie said quietly. 'But running is still a reflex for me when men get angry. I can't help it. The two years Mum was married to that man were terrifying for Chrissie and me.'

'Did he hit you as well?' Cesare growled in disgust, appalled that he could have, however unwittingly, frightened her.

'He tried to a couple of times but he was drunk and clumsy and we were fast on our feet,' Lizzie confided. 'Let's not talk about it. It's in the past. But I should make one thing clear...' She hesitated. 'I'm only willing to talk about Andrew if you're willing to talk about Serafina.'

'And exactly who has been talking to you?' Cesare demanded, a muscle pulling taut at the corner of his stern, handsome mouth.

'Your grandmother mentioned her...and I'm curious too,' Lizzie confessed while she walked into the dressing room in search of a nightdress. Shedding the towel behind the door, she slipped it on, catching a glimpse of herself in a tall mirror. What remained of her fake glamour had evaporated in the long bath she had taken. The moist atmosphere had added frizz to her formerly smooth tresses and she suppressed a sigh. Cesare was getting the *real* Lizzie Whitaker on this particular night.

Emerging from the dressing room with Archie at her heels, she tried not to visibly shrink from Cesare's acute appraisal. The silk nightie was long and, to her, the very antithesis of sexy because it revealed neither leg nor cleavage. Her face coloured as she stilled for a split second, disturbingly aware of the intensity of that assessment from his smouldering dark golden eyes. A wave of heat shimmied over her, settling at the tips of her breasts and between her thighs in a tingling, throbbing awareness that mortified her. She knew he was thinking about sex. She also knew that he was making *her* think about sex. And she didn't know how he did it. Hormonal awareness was like an invisible electric current lacing the atmosphere.

Cesare watched the candlelight throw Lizzie's slender legs into view behind the thin silk and his mouth ran dry while the rest of him ran hot and heavy. Her pert breasts shimmying below the material in the most stimulating way, she curled up at the foot of the bed and reached for a plate of snacks. 'So, who goes first?'

'I will,' Cesare surprised himself by saying. Although he had initially been disconcerted by her demand he was now more amused that she should want to travel that far back into his past. It simply irritated him, though, that his grandmother was willing to credit that a youthful love affair gone wrong could still have any influence over him.

'Serafina…it's a beautiful name,' Lizzie remarked thoughtfully.

'She is very beautiful,' Cesare admitted, quietly contemplative as he sprawled back indolently against the headboard of the bed. 'We were students together. I was doing business, she was doing business law. It was first love, all very intense stuff.'

Lizzie watched him grimace at that admission. 'My first love was a poster of a boy-band member on the wall,' she confided in some embarrassment.

'A poster would've been a safer option for me. I fell hard and fast and I wanted to marry Serafina. She said we were too young and she was right,' he conceded wryly. 'She was always ambitious and I assumed that I'd have to start at the bottom of the business ladder. But then I made a stock-market killing and took over my first company and my prospects improved. Serafina started work at an upmarket legal practice with some very rich…and influential clients…'

'And at that point, you were still together?' Lizzie prompted when the silence dragged, his delivery becoming noticeably less smooth.

'Very much so. We were living together. Second week in her new job, Serafina met Matteo Ruffini and he invited her out to dinner with a view to offering her the opportunity to work on his substantial account.' His beautiful mouth took on a sardonic slant. 'Suddenly she became unavailable to me, working late in the evening, too busy to join me for lunch.'

His tension was unhidden. Lizzie registered that Serafina had hurt him and hurt him deep because he still couldn't talk about the woman with indifference. 'She was seeing Matteo?'

'*Sì*…and the moment *Prince* Matteo proposed, I was history. He had everything she had ever wanted. Social position, a title and immense wealth. The only flaw in his perfection was that she was twenty-five and he was seventy-five.'

'Good grief! That's a huge age gap!' Lizzie exclaimed. 'Did she tell you she'd fallen in love with him?'

'No. Possibly that would have been easier to accept, if not believe. No, she told me that he was just too good a catch to turn down and that if she contrived to give him a son and heir, she'd be rich and blessed for the rest of her life,' Cesare breathed with derision. 'I realised I'd never really known her. It crushed my faith in women.'

'Of course it did,' Lizzie agreed, the nails of one hand biting into her palm while odd disconnected emotions flailed her, particularly when she found herself thinking aggressive thoughts about the woman who had broken Cesare's heart. She had read him *so* wrong when they first met. He had been prepared to leap into the commitment and responsibility of marriage at a very young age. Clearly, he had genuinely loved Serafina and yet she had betrayed him in the worst possible way when she chose a life of rich privilege over love.

'Andrew?' Cesare pressed in turn.

'He was my best friend growing up. We had so much in common we should've been a perfect match and we stayed great friends although he never actually asked me out until I was in my twenties. I was already in love with him…at least I *thought* it was love,' she said ruefully. 'Everybody assumed we would be great together and when he asked me to marry him, Dad was ecstatic. I said yes but I wanted us to just date for a while.' Her face paling, she studied her tightly clasped hands.

'It was in private that Andrew and I didn't work out.'

'Obviously you didn't sleep with him,' Cesare murmured softly, watching the fragile bones of her face tighten, the vulnerable curve of her mouth tense, feeling his own chest tighten in response.

'No, I just didn't want to sleep with him,' she admitted in an awkward rush. 'I froze every time he got close and he said I was frigid but I didn't find him attractive that way. I thought I had a real problem with being touched. That's why I wouldn't date anyone after him and why I never blamed him for turning to Esther.'

'You don't have *any* kind of a problem,' Cesare asserted with quiet confidence. 'You were inexperienced; maybe he was as well—'

'No,' Lizzie broke in, running back through her memories while remembered feelings of inadequacy and regret engulfed her.

Yet even before she had fallen asleep in the bath she had realised that her enjoyment of Cesare's attentions had shed a comforting light on the past, which had always troubled her. Her only *real* problem with Andrew had been that he had always felt like the brother she had never had. She could see things as they had been now, not as she might have wished them to be: sadly, there had been zero sexual attraction on her side. She had sincerely cared for Andrew but he had always felt more like a good friend than a potential lover. When she compared how she had reacted from the first moment with Cesare, she could clearly see the difference and finally understand that what had happened with Andrew was not her fault.

'I liked and appreciated him but I never wanted him that way,' Lizzie admitted with regret. 'I still feel guilty about it because I was too inexperienced to realise that he was just the wrong man for me…and my rejections hurt him.'

'He seems happy enough now.' Cesare toyed with another piece of chicken.

Encouraged to think that further treats were in the pipeline, Archie got up on his haunches and begged.

'Oh, my goodness, look what he's doing!' Lizzie exclaimed, sitting forward with wide eyes to watch her pet. 'He can beg…I didn't even know he could *do* that.'

Cesare rewarded Archie with the chicken because he had made his mistress smile and laugh.

'Of course, I've never fed him like that. If he'd come to me for food when I was eating my father would have called that bad behaviour and he would have blamed Archie. I kept Archie outside most of the time.'

'I suspect Archie would've been clever enough to keep a low profile around your dad,' Cesare surmised.

'Did you ever have a pet?'

'I would have liked one when I was a kid,' Cesare confided. 'But I was constantly moving between my grandmother's home and Goffredo's apartment and a pet wasn't viable.'

'Did you organise all this food?' she asked, smothering a yawn.

'The staff are in bed. I don't expect service here late at night,' he told her quietly. 'I emptied the refrigerator.'

'And let Archie up to lure me out of the bathroom,' Lizzie guessed, settling their discarded plates on the low table and clambering in the far side of the bed to say apologetically, 'I'm tired.'

'Brides aren't supposed to get tired, particularly not when they've been lazing in the bath for hours,' Cesare informed her, amusement dancing in his dark golden eyes.

He could still steal her breath away at one

glance, she acknowledged wearily as she closed her eyes. It was, as he had termed it, 'just sex' and she had to learn to see that side of their relationship in the same casual light. She wondered if that would be a challenge because she was already drifting dangerously close to liking him.

'Archie can sleep under the bed,' Cesare decreed. 'He's not sharing it with us.'

'We can't do anything, you know,' she muttered in a sudden embarrassed surge, her cheeks colouring. 'I'm…I'm sore…'

'It's not a problem.'

Relieved, she smiled and closed her eyes. As he stripped by the side of the bed Cesare studied her relaxed features and thought, *Mission accomplished, honeymoon back on track.* It was the same way he handled problems at work, mentally ticking off items on a to-do list while always seeking the most successful conclusion. But as he slid into bed beside Lizzie he reached for her and it wasn't a pre-programmed task. He reasoned that she was a very restless sleeper and if he left her free to move around she would annoy him.

Strangely enough, he acknowledged, in spite of the bathroom shenanigans, she hadn't annoyed him once. But then she wasn't the greedy, grasping type of woman he had deemed her to be. Why had he been so biased? After all, he had a stepmother, a grandmother and three sisters, none of whom were rich *or* avaricious. Had he deliberately sought out lovers who only cared about his wealth? And if he was guilty of that, had it been because he genuinely only needed carefree sex with a woman? Or because he preferred to avoid the possibility of anything more serious developing? Almost ten years had passed since Serafina had waltzed down the aisle to her prince. He refused to think that she had burned him so badly that he had declined to risk getting deeply involved with anyone else. Yet he hadn't even got an engagement or a live-in relationship under his belt during those ten long years.

In the darkness, Cesare's wide, sensual mouth framed a silent but vehemently felt swear word. He did not appreciate the oddity of having such thoughts about the sort of thing he had never ever felt the need to think about before. It was that ring on his wedding finger that was getting to him, he brooded impatiently. It was feeling married and possibly just a tiny bit trapped...with Archie snoring beside the bed and Lizzie nestled up against him like a second skin.

Just like him, she was in this marriage for the end game and the prize, he reminded himself squarely. It wasn't a normal marriage but, if they planned to conceive a child, the marriage had to work on a daily basis and why should physical intimacy always lead to a closer involvement than he wanted? The answer was that sex didn't need to lead to anything more complex, he reminded himself stubbornly, certainly nothing that would break his rules of never getting more closely involved with a woman. And it was no wonder that he was feeling unsettled when he was in such unfamiliar territory. He hadn't tried to please a woman since Serafina and he wasn't going to make a fool of himself trying to please Lizzie, was he?

Archie's snores filtered up in direct disagreement.

CHAPTER EIGHT

CESARE GLANCED AT his wife and then at the party of men watching her every move in a pantomime version of dropped jaws as she alighted from his Ferrari. She was a lissom figure in a turquoise sundress, her gorgeous silvery mane blowing back from her delicately flushed face in the breeze, her shapely legs tapering down to impossibly delicate ankles and high-heeled sandals. He pushed up his sunglasses and gave the men a warning look before closing his hand round Lizzie's in a display of all-Italian male possessiveness that he could not resist.

Lizzie sank down at the table in the *piazza* and the waiter was at their side within seconds, doubtless drawn by one glimpse of Cesare's sleek sophistication. He had an air of hauteur and command that got them fast service everywhere they went and it was so inbred in him to expect immediate attention that he rarely even noticed the fact, although she was very sure he would notice if he didn't receive it.

Now she feasted her attention on his lean bronzed face. She was magnetised by his stunning dark golden eyes as they rested on her and wondered what he was thinking. She was *always* wondering what he was thinking, had to bite her tongue not to ask, but it was hardly surprising that she was living in a state of constant befuddlement because their business-based marriage of convenience had become something else entirely…at least for *her*…

They had now been in Italy for a solid month. Cesare had made several business trips. He had flown his family *and* Chrissie in to visit for one weekend and the two days had passed in a whirlwind of chattering liveliness and warmth. Lizzie had never been so happy before and it scared her because she knew she was nourishing hopes that would ultimately lead to disappointment and the stark biting pain of rejection. *What? Only possibly?* jibed her more truthful self. Lizzie's emotions had got involved the very first night they'd slept together and she'd wakened in the morning to find herself secure in Cesare's arms.

For four whole weeks she had been living an idyllic life with an attentive husband, who was also a passionate lover, by her side. He had taken her out sightseeing, shopping, out to dinner in sun-baked *piazzas*, fashionable squares, and to wander through old churches lit by candles and the sunlight piercing the stained-glass windows. Today they had walked the seventeenth-century ramparts of Lucca. Her fingers toyed momentarily with the slender gold watch encircling her wrist, her most recent gift. If he went on a trip or even noticed that she lacked something he considered essential, he bought it for her. He was incredibly generous in bed and out of it. He was curious about her, knew everything there was to know about her childhood. His interest was intoxicating because she had never seen herself as being particularly interesting. In fact, being the focus of attention of a very handsome, entertaining male had made her see herself in a kinder, warmer light.

In truth, when Cesare Sabatino was faking being a husband, he faked with the skill and panache of a professional, she conceded ruefully. He hadn't asked her to fall in love with him. It wouldn't occur to him that bringing an ordinary woman out to beautiful Tuscany and treating her like a much appreciated, highly desirable wife while keeping her in luxury might turn her head. But Lizzie knew her head had been thoroughly turned. She found him fascinating. He was a spellbinding mix of rapier-sharp intellect and disconcerting emotional depth and, of course, she had fallen head over heels for him. Archie now rejoiced in a collar with his name picked out in diamonds and a four-poster bed of his own. How could she *not* love the man who had given her adored pet those quite unnecessary, ridiculously expensive but deeply touching things?

And the result was that now she was terrified of falling pregnant, fearing that that announcement would ensure that their marriage cooled back down to a businesslike arrangement in which Cesare would expect her to be terribly civilised and behave as if she didn't give a damn about him. Within days of the wedding she had had the proof that she had not yet conceived and Cesare had just laughed and said that they had all the time in the world, as if it truly didn't matter to him if it took months to reach that goal.

'What if there's something wrong with one of us and it doesn't happen?' she had asked him anxiously.

He had shrugged and suggested that they give it a year before seeking medical advice. If for some reason having a child turned out not to be possible, they would deal with it when it happened, Cesare had told her fatalistically while urging her not to stress about getting pregnant.

'I hope you've got something special lined up to wear tonight,' Cesare mused over their wine. 'It's a real fashion parade.'

'I thought it was a charity do.'

'In Italy such events are always fashion parades.'

'I have at least four long dresses to choose from,' Lizzie reminded him. 'I won't let you down. Don't worry about it.'

'*Ma no*...certainly not,' Cesare cut in, stroking a long forefinger soothingly over her hand where it curled on the table top. 'You always look fantastic, *gioia mia*. Why would I be worried about you letting me down?'

'I'm not part of your world and I never will be. It's a challenge for me to put on fancy clothes and pretend I'm something I'm not,' Lizzie admitted in an undertone.

'You only need to be yourself. You have two, no, three...' he adjusted reflectively, amusement gleaming in his gilded gaze '... advantages.'

'Which are?'

'Beauty and class and my ring on your finger,' Cesare completed with cynical cool. 'I'm a powerful man. You will be treated with respect and courtesy.'

An involuntary grin lit up Lizzie's face and she laughed, biting back foolish words of love. What an embarrassment it would be if she were to lose control of her tongue around him now! After all, he was playing a very sophisticated game with her, utilising his charm and a whole host of other extraordinary gifts to make their marriage work as if it were a real marriage. If she were to suddenly confess how she felt about him, he would be embarrassed and appalled to learn that she didn't know how to play the same game.

'We should head back soon,' she commented unevenly.

'Would that leave us time for an hour or so in bed?' Cesare sprang upright, dropping a large-denomination note down on top of the bill, smouldering dark eyes flashing over her with a sexual intensity that never failed to thrill.

'Again?' There was a slight gasp in her low-pitched response because she had yet to adapt to Cesare's high-voltage libido. He seemed to want her all the time, no matter where she was, no matter what she was wearing or what she was doing. She thought he was possibly a little oversexed but she didn't complain because she always wanted him too and, in any case, the whole point of their marriage was for her to conceive a child.

A light hand resting in the shallow indentation of her spine, Cesare urged her back to the Ferrari. As she clambered in beside him he turned his head and closed a hard hand into the tumble of her hair to hold her fast while he kissed her. His mouth was hungry and hot and erotic on hers and every sense was on overdrive by the time he freed her again and started up the car.

The air conditioning cooled her over-heated skin but the ache throbbing between her thighs was far less controllable. Cesare skimmed up her skirt to bare her thighs. 'I like looking at your legs, especially when I know I'm about to part them,' he husked soft and low, laughing when her cheeks flamed.

Early evening, Lizzie inspected her reflection in a black shimmering dress that delineated her slender figure with a spare elegance that appealed to her. She was learning what she liked and didn't like in her wardrobe and she didn't like fussy trims or frills or neon-bright colours that seemed to swallow her alive.

Warmth speckled her cheeks as she thought about the intimacy of the late-afternoon hours. She moved slowly in her heels, a touch of tenderness at the heart of her reminding her of Cesare's passionate energy between the sheets. In bed, sensual excitement ruled her entirely and she was enjoying every moment of exploring that brave new world.

Even so the image that lingered longest was of Cesare, lithe and bronzed and breathtakingly beautiful, relaxing back against the tumbled pillows and finally admitting how very relieved he was that Athene was now well on the road to recovery, having initially suffered a setback in the aftermath of her cardiac surgery. For days, he had tried to pretend he wasn't worried sick even though Lizzie had watched him freeze at every phone call, fearful of receiving bad news. That he had finally abandoned that macho pretence of unconcern to share his true feelings with Lizzie had meant a lot to her. She valued the little signs that revealed that Cesare was behaving more and more like one half of a couple rather than an independent, entirely separate entity. They had visited his grandmother in her convalescent clinic in Rome several times and Athene's sparkling personality even in a hospital bed and her strong affection for Cesare had touched Lizzie's heart.

In the morning they were flying out to Lionos and one day after that Athene was coming out to join them. Cesare had married Lizzie purely to gain that right to bring his grandmother out for a stay on the island and Lizzie regularly reminded herself of that unflattering reality. But she was looking forward almost as much as Athene was to seeing Lionos, which the older woman had described in such charmed terms. She only hoped that the enhancements engineered by the imperturbable Primo lived up to Cesare's expectations.

A limousine ferried Cesare and Lizzie to the venue for the charity benefit in Florence. It was being held in a vast mansion with every window lit and crowds of paparazzi waiting on the pavement to take photographs of the guests arriving. Lizzie froze in surprise when they were targeted, belatedly appreciating that she was married to a male who, when in his homeland, received the attention worthy of a celebrity for his looks and spectacular business accomplishments.

'Did you enjoy having your photo taken?' Cesare asked.

'No, not at all. I didn't feel glossy enough for the occasion,' she confided.

'But you spent ages getting ready,' Cesare countered with all the incomprehension of a male who had merely showered and shaved before donning a dinner jacket.

Her hazel gaze roving swiftly over the level of extreme grooming clearly practised by the other female guests, Lizzie suppressed a rueful sigh. She didn't look perfect and she knew it, reckoned she should have foreseen that the attentions of a hairstylist and a make-up artist would be necessary. But then how important was her image to Cesare? Did he really care? Or would he soon be comparing her, to her detriment, to the women who had preceded her in his bed? Lizzie had done her homework on the Internet and she was uneasily aware that in recent years Cesare had spent a lot of time in the company of fashion and beauty models, invariably the very image of feminine perfection. Possibly she needed to make more of an effort, she conceded, uncomfortable with the comparisons she was making.

As they were surrounded by the leading lights in the charity committee of which Cesare was a director, the crowd parted and an exquisite brunette, wearing a very fitted pink dress overlaid with a see-through chiffon layer that simply accentuated her stupendous curves, approached them. Cesare performed the introduction. 'Our hostess, Princess Serafina Ruffini…Serafina, my wife, Lizzie.'

'Welcome to my home, Lizzie.' Serafina air kissed her on both cheeks and gave her a wide, seemingly sincere smile.

Shock winged through Lizzie and she was furious that Cesare hadn't warned her that the benefit was being held at his former girlfriend's home. Impervious to her mood and the manner in which her hand clenched tensely on his arm, Cesare talked about cancer research to an older man who seemed to be a doctor while Lizzie made awkward conversation with his wife, who spoke very little English. Italian lessons were going to be a must in the near future, Lizzie promised herself. Her attention crept back to Serafina, holding court on the other side of the room with a lively group who frequently broke into laughter.

Cesare had described his ex as *very* beautiful and he had not been kidding. Serafina had almond-shaped dark eyes, skin like clotted cream, a wealth of dark tumbling curls and one of those enviable cupid's-bow scarlet mouths that men always seemed to go mad for. And, more worryingly, Serafina appeared to move in the same social milieu as Cesare, possibly to the extent that Cesare had not even felt it necessary to mention that Lizzie would be meeting her that very evening. For goodness' sake, he broke up with her almost ten years ago, Lizzie reminded herself impatiently. How likely was it that he was still hankering after what he had lost?

In conversation with one of the organisers, who spoke great English, Lizzie learned how indebted the charity felt to Serafina, not only for her recent decision to become their patroness but also for allowing her magnificent home to be used for a fundraising benefit. La Principessa, she learned, was worth a small fortune to the charity in terms of the PR and publicity she would bring their cause, which was raising sufficient funds to open a new hospice for terminally ill children.

It was very warm in the crowded room and perspiration began to bead on Lizzie's brow. She glanced longingly across the room to where several sets of doors stood open onto an outside terrace. As she stood there, a glass of water clasped in one hand, a sick sensation composed of both dizziness and nausea washed over her, leaving her pale.

'Excuse me, I'm warm and I think I'll step outside for a few minutes,' she told her companion and turned away, wondering if she should be taking refuge in the cloakroom instead, but praying that the cooler night air would revive her.

The terrace was furnished with tables and chairs, and lights and candles held the darkness at bay. Lizzie took a seat, gratefully feeling the clamminess of her skin and the faint sickness recede again and breathing the fresh air in deep while she wondered if she was simply tired or if, indeed, she could be in the very earliest stage of a pregnancy. Wonder at that faint suspicion curved her mouth into a ready smile but delight at the prospect was swiftly tempered by fear of what such a development might mean to her relationship with Cesare. Would he back off from their current intimacy? Would he stop treating her like a real wife?

'I saw you come outside,' a female voice said lightly. 'I thought we should get acquainted. I've known Cesare for so many years,' Serafina Ruffini told her with apparent warmth. 'You haven't been married long, have you?'

'No, only for a month,' Lizzie admitted, struggling to maintain her relaxed attitude in the face of Serafina's shrewdly assessing gaze.

'My husband, Matteo, passed away last year. I'm fortunate to have my seven-year-old son to comfort me,' Serafina confided.

'I'm sorry for your loss,' Lizzie murmured, guiltily dismayed at the news that the brunette was a widow. 'It must be hard for you and your son.'

'We're getting used to being a twosome.' Serafina signalled a waiter hovering by the door with an imperious gesture wholly in keeping with her rather royal air of command. 'Champagne?'

'No, thanks.' Lizzie smoothed a fingertip round the rim of her glass of water while smiling valiantly as the brunette continued to watch her closely.

The champagne was served with a flourish. Serafina leant back in her upholstered seat. 'Of course, you'll know about my history with Cesare…'

Lizzie stiffened. 'Yes.'

'How honest can I be with you?'

'As honest as you like but I don't think Cesare would like us talking about him behind his back,' Lizzie opined quietly.

'He's an Italian male with a healthy ego.' Serafina laughed. 'Being wanted and appreciated by women is the bread of life for him.'

'Is that why you didn't marry him?' Lizzie heard herself ask helplessly. 'You believed he would be a womaniser?'

'No, not at all. I married for security. I didn't grow up like Cesare in a comfortable middle-class home,' Serafina confided, startling Lizzie with her frankness. 'I came from a poor background and worked very hard for everything I got and I had a great fear of being poor again. Matteo was a proven success while Cesare was only starting out in the business world. I loved Cesare but I'm afraid that the security which Matteo offered me was irresistible.'

Thoroughly disconcerted by that unembarrassed explanation, Lizzie murmured without expression, 'You made the right decision for you.'

Serafina saluted her with her glass in gratitude. 'I believe that I did but once I saw how well Cesare was doing in business, I naturally wished I had had more faith in him.'

'I expect you did,' Lizzie conceded tautly. 'But you had a husband and a child by then and everything had changed.'

'But I still never stopped loving Cesare and, I warn you now, I intend to get him back.'

'You expect me to listen to this?' Lizzie asked, beginning to rise from her seat, having heard enough of Serafina's self-absorbed excuses.

'No, don't go,' Serafina urged impatiently. 'I'm sorry if I shocked you but I want you to understand that, right now, Cesare is set on punishing me for what I did to him almost ten years ago.'

Involuntarily, Lizzie settled back in her seat. '*Punishing* you?'

'What else could he have been doing when he married you? He married you to *hurt* me. Here I am, finally free and available and he marries you. What sense does that make?'

'Has it occurred to you that maybe he's

over you and doesn't want you back?' Lizzie asked helplessly, provoked by the brunette's conviction that she would always be Cesare's most desirable option and reminding herself that she was supposed to be Cesare's real wife and should be reacting accordingly to Serafina's little spiel. 'Your affair ended a long time ago.'

'You *never* forget your first love,' Serafina argued with ringing conviction. 'He's even living in the house we planned together.'

'What house?'

'The farmhouse. We first saw it as students. It was a wet night and we made love in the barn,' Serafina admitted, a rapt look in her bright eyes as Lizzie hastily dropped her lashes to conceal her expression.

Too much information, Lizzie was thinking anxiously, an odd pain clenching her down deep inside. She could not bear to think of Cesare making love with Serafina and could have happily tossed Serafina's champagne into her sensually abstracted face. Serafina had married her older man for security and wealth while still loving and wanting Cesare. Lizzie did not think the brunette had any right to expect to turn the clock back or indeed any excuse to risk upsetting Cesare's new wife with intimate and threatening images from the past she had once shared with him.

'Even though I was already married to Matteo, Cesare still bought the farmhouse as soon as it came on the market,' Serafina told her smugly. 'Look across the valley in the evening from the pool terrace and you will see the Ruffini *palazzo* blazing with lights on the hillside. He wants me back, Lizzie, he's simply too proud to admit it yet.'

'I don't think he would've married me if that was his intention,' Lizzie commented in a deflated tone.

'Oh, I guessed that he married you to get that stupid island back into the family,' Serafina retorted with a wry little laugh and she shrugged. 'I don't care about that. Your marriage is temporary and I'll be waiting when he decides to forgive me.'

'Whatever,' Lizzie mumbled, thrusting her chair back and rising. 'You can hardly expect me to wish you luck with my husband and I really don't understand why you wanted to talk to me in the first place.'

'Because you can make things a lot easier for all three of us by quietly stepping back the minute Cesare admits that he wants his freedom back,' the princess pointed out smoothly. 'If it's a question of money.'

'No, I don't *need* money and I can't be bribed!' Lizzie parried grittily, her cheeks reddening. 'I wish I could say it was nice meeting you...but it would be a lie.'

'You're a farmer's daughter with no education. Surely you don't believe you have what it takes to hold a man like Cesare's interest?' Serafina fired back with a raised brow. 'Cesare and I belong together.'

CHAPTER NINE

LIZZIE COMPRESSED HER LIPS, said nothing and walked back indoors.

A pounding headache had developed at the base of her skull. How she got through what remained of the evening, she had no idea, but she smiled so much her mouth felt numb and she made polite conversation until she wanted to scream. She was angry with Cesare for ever loving a woman as selfish and grasping as Serafina. Serafina only wanted Cesare now because he had built up an empire worth billions. Nevertheless a few of her remarks stayed with Lizzie like a bruise that refused to heal.

'You never forget your first love. He married you to hurt me. Cesare and I belong together.'

And who was she to assume that that wasn't true? Cesare had never dreamt of regaining the island of Lionos in the way his father and grandmother had. Never having seen it, he had never learned to care for it and could probably well afford to buy his own island should that have been his wish. Was it possible that Cesare had been willing to go through with marrying Lizzie because he had a stronger motive? A desire to punish Serafina for her betrayal all those years ago? *Revenge?* Certainly that was how the princess had interpreted his behaviour of getting married just at the point when she was finally free again. Exasperated by the pointless thoughts going round and round in her sore head, Lizzie tried to blank them out by acknowledging that she knew no more about what Cesare felt for Serafina than she knew about what he felt for herself.

'You've scarcely spoken since we left the benefit,' Cesare commented as the limo drew up outside the farmhouse. He had noticed that she had seemed unusually animated throughout the evening. That had proved a surprise when he had assumed she might feel the need to cling to him in such exclusive and high-powered company. When she failed to demonstrate any desire to cling, instead of being relieved he had felt strangely irked and could not explain why. He had always felt stifled by women who clung to him. He had always valued independence and spirit in a woman more than feminine weakness and soft words of flattery.

Yet when the spirited and independent woman whom he had once loved had approached him at the benefit for a private word, he had been totally turned off by the experience, he acknowledged grimly.

'I'm very tired,' Lizzie said stiffly.

Cesare followed her into the bedroom, unzipping her dress without being asked. Lizzie let the dress glide down to her feet, stepped out of it and, regal as a queen in her underwear, walked into the bathroom without turning her head even to look at him.

He knew when he was getting the silent treatment. She was sulking and that was childish. He had never had any patience for sulks. He pulled a pair of jeans out of a drawer and stripped off his suit. Casually clad, he noted the beady little eyes watching him from below the canopy of the four-poster pet bed and surrendered. 'Come on, Archie... time for something to eat...'

Archie limped across the floor. The cast had been removed from his broken leg only the day before but Archie still thought he was a three-legged dog and had yet to trust the fourth leg to take his weight again. Cesare scooped the little dog up at the top of the stairs and carried him down to the kitchen where he maintained a one-way dialogue with Archie while feeding them both as he raided the fridge.

Teeth gritted, Lizzie emerged from the bathroom to a frustratingly empty bedroom. She had decided that it was beyond cowardly not to ask Cesare why he hadn't warned her that the benefit was being staged at his ex-girlfriend's home. She had not been prepared for that confrontation and was convinced she would have made a more serious effort to look her very best had she known she would be meeting the gorgeous brunette. The problem was that she was jealous, she acknowledged ruefully, green and raw and hurting with ferocious jealousy. She looked out of the landing window at the dark silhouette of the old stone barn and her heart clenched as if it had been squeezed dry. Cesare had made love to Serafina there, love, *not sex*. He had loved Serafina, cared about her, *wanted* to marry her. Yet Serafina had turned her back on his love in favour of wealth and social status. Having achieved those staples, she now wanted Cesare back.

Pulling a silky wrap on over a nightdress, Lizzie headed downstairs. Cesare was sprawled on a sofa in the airy living room. In worn jeans and an unbuttoned blue shirt, he was a long sleek bronzed figure and heartbreakingly beautiful. Her heart hammered out a responsive and nervous tattoo as she paused in the doorway.

'Why didn't you tell me?' she asked abruptly.

Cesare always avoided dramatic scenes with women and walking out on the risk of one came as naturally as breathing to him. One glance at Lizzie's set, angry face and the eyes gleaming like green witch fire in her flushed face was sufficient to warn him of what was coming. Springing lithely upright, he strolled out past her and swiped the car keys off the cabinet in the hall. 'I'm going for a drive…don't wait up for me. I'll be late,' he spelled out flatly.

Taken aback, Lizzie moved fast to place herself in his path to the front door. 'Are you serious?'

'Perfectly. I don't want to argue with you, *cara*. I'm not in the mood. We're flying to Lionos tomorrow and Athene will be joining us. That is enough of a challenge for the present.'

It was a shock for Lizzie to register how cold the smooth, perfect planes of his lean dark face could look. His spectacular eyes were veiled by his thick lashes, his superb bone structure taut, his shapely mouth, defined by a dark shadow of stubble, a hard line of restraint. Alarm bells sounded in her head. 'You could've warned me that we were going to Serafina's house and that she would be our hostess.'

'I am not going to argue with you about Serafina,' Cesare asserted, his jawline clenching hard as granite.

'I'm *not* arguing with you,' Lizzie reasoned curtly. 'And why won't you discuss her with me?'

Velvet black lashes flew up on scorching golden eyes. 'She's none of your business, nothing to do with you.'

Lizzie flinched and leant back against the door to stay upright. She felt like someone trying to walk a tightrope in the dark and she was terrified of falling. 'She spent ten minutes talking to me outside on the terrace and made me feel very much as if she was my business.'

Feverish colour laced his incredible cheek-bones. '*You*...discussed me with...*her*?' he framed wrathfully.

Lizzie found it interesting that, instead of being flattered as Serafina had suggested, Cesare was absolutely outraged by the idea. 'What do you think?' She hesitated, hovering between him and the door. 'I only wanted to know why you didn't mention that she would be entertaining us.'

Cesare ground his perfect white teeth together because he *had* thought of mentioning it, only to run aground on the recollection that theirs was not a normal marriage. They were not in a relationship where he was bound to make such personal explanations, were they? He focused on Lizzie's pale face on which colour stood out only on her cheeks. She looked hurt. He saw that hurt and in-stinctively recoiled from it, frustration rip-pling through him. He didn't want to share what had happened earlier that evening with Lizzie, not only because it would rouse her suspicions, but also because it was tacky and he *refused* to bring that tacky element into what had proved to be a glorious honeymoon.

'Serafina is very much part of the local scenery. Many of my friends are also hers.

I have no reason to avoid her. Seeing her is no big deal,' he delineated stiffly, reluctantly, willing to throw that log on the fire if it satisfied her and closed the subject.

'I don't believe you,' Lizzie whispered unhappily. 'If it had been no big deal, you would've mentioned it.'

'You know me so well?' he derided.

Lizzie paled even more. 'I thought I did.'

Cesare closed his hands firmly to her ribcage and lifted her bodily away from the door.

'If you walk out, I'm not going to Lionos with you!' Lizzie flung the worst threat she could think to make in an effort to stop him in his tracks.

'In what fantasy world are you living that you think you can threaten me?' Cesare breathed, freezing with the door ajar so that cooler night air filtered in to cool her now clammy skin.

'I only wanted you to explain.'

'I have nothing to explain,' Cesare parried drily. 'But you will definitely be telling me at some point what Serafina said to you.'

'Honesty has to be a two-way thing to work. We've been living like a married couple.'

'Because we *are* married.'

'You know what I mean...' Lizzie hesitated, reluctant to probe deeper but driven by turbulent emotional forces she could not suppress. 'You've been treating me as though I'm really your wife.'

There it was—the truth Cesare had hoped to evade because he didn't know *how* that had happened, didn't know what to say to her, didn't even know how he felt about that development. Why did women always have to drag unmentionable issues out into the open and do them to death at a time of their choosing? How the hell had he got himself into such an untenable situation? He had started out fine, he acknowledged broodingly, laying down the rules, seeing what made sense, knowing what he should not do lest it lead to exactly this situation. And somehow it had all gone to hell in a hand basket in spite of *all* that careful pre-planning, *all* that practical knowhow and knowledge of the female sex. And here he was trapped as he had never wanted to be trapped...

'I want to know what Serafina said to you.'

'That she wants you back, that you married me to punish her, that I wasn't educated enough to hold you... Oh, yes,' Lizzie recounted and then, with a ghastly attempt at an amused smile, added, 'and that this was your mutual dream house, planned by you both on the wet night you made love in the barn…'

Cesare's eyes flashed flaming gold, his outrage unconcealed. He closed a hard hand to the edge of the door as if to emphasise the fact that he was still leaving. '*Madonna diavolo!* She shouldn't have involved you in this.'

At those words, at that suggestion that there was an involvement that she was unaware of, Lizzie swore her heart cracked right down the middle. 'No,' she agreed woodenly, because it was true.

Cesare steeled himself. He knew he had to speak, could not comprehend why ESP was suddenly warning him to shut up and say nothing. 'We don't have a genuine marriage. We are not a couple in the true sense of the word. We both know that…'

He paused as if he was hoping she would leap in and say something but Lizzie couldn't have found her voice had her life depended on it. At that moment she felt as if her life's blood were draining away in a pool on the floor and that dramatic image made her feel dizzy.

'I'm going to bed,' she mumbled, knowing that she was lying, knowing that sleep had never been further from her mind, but it seemed so incredibly important in that silence to act as if she were still able to function normally even if it was a complete lie to try and save face.

'This is all my fault,' Cesare breathed in a roughened undertone. 'Don't think I'm not aware of that. I shouldn't have brought something as volatile as sex into the equation.'

'And you were still doing it…only a few hours ago,' she framed unevenly.

Unusually indecisive, Cesare hovered in the rushing silence. Archie was looking at him from across the hall as if he had two heads, which absolutely had to be his imagination playing tricks on him, he reasoned wildly. He felt sick, he felt bad, he felt… No, he was being dangerously emotional and he knew what emotion did to him: it made him irrational and reckless and he wasn't going to go there again…*ever*! He was taking the right approach in correcting a serious mistake before it did any more damage. Aside of that aspect, they were both consenting adults.

'So, it's back to the business arrangement,' Lizzie assumed in a tight little voice.

'I think that would be wiser, don't you?'

Not recognising that cold, detached intonation, Lizzie finally dared to look at him again. He was poised by the door, devastatingly handsome, a long slice of bare brown torso showing between the parted edges of his shirt, tight jeans defining long, powerful thighs and lean hips. Slowly she raised her gaze, determined to be brave, determined to hold on to her pride even though he had rejected her in the worst possible and most hurtfully humiliating way. He had made it clear where he stood and she supposed that brutal honesty was for the best.

'Goodnight,' Lizzie said quietly and she turned on her heel.

In a split second the front door closed and he was gone. The Ferrari engine growled to life and she literally ran out to the terrace above the pool, frantically determined to see if she could pick out the Ruffini *palazzo* on the hillside. And there it was, a big white classical building lit up like a fairground. She had noticed it before but had never thought to ask about it. Now she watched the lights of Cesare's car heading down into the valley and she stood and she stood, arms wrapped defensively round herself while she waited to see if her very worst suspicions were correct.

At such a distance, she could not have been a hundred per cent certain but she was convinced that it was the Ferrari that she saw heading up the long, winding, steep drive to the *palazzo*. Cesare was going straight to see Serafina. Lizzie was in shock. Perhaps he had been seeing the other woman all along; Lizzie hadn't been keeping tabs on him everywhere he went. It seemed pretty obvious to her that Cesare had a dark side and more secrets than she had ever had cause to suspect and she had been ignorant and irresponsible and very naive not to smell a rat sooner...but it wasn't much good or any comfort to feel wise *after* the event, was it?

CHAPTER TEN

THE FOLLOWING MORNING, with her heart beating very fast, Lizzie studied a test wand, relieved that she had taken the opportunity to discreetly buy a pregnancy kit some weeks earlier.

And there it was straight away, the result she had both feared and craved: she was pregnant. It changed everything, she acknowledged in shock, and she walked out to the bedroom and unlocked the door she had locked the night before. Cesare would need access to his clothes but had she cared about that last night when her dream world had collapsed about her ears? No, she had not.

But now that she knew for sure that she was carrying Cesare's baby, she had to look to the future and beyond the business agreement they had originally made. She could not afford to be at odds with her child's father.

That would only foster resentment between them and their child would suffer in that scenario. Unfortunately that meant that she had to be a bigger person than she felt like being just at that moment. She had to rise above what had happened, bury the personal aspect and stick to the rules from here on in.

He'd broken her heart. Well, she'd recovered from Andrew; she would eventually recover from Cesare. Of course, she had never loved Andrew the way she loved Cesare; consequently getting over Cesare would be more of a challenge. Andrew had hurt her self-esteem and damaged her trust but Cesare had torn her heart out. To think of living even one day without Cesare somewhere nearby tore her apart, teaching her how weak and vulnerable her emotions had made her.

Yes, Lizzie acknowledged, tidying her hair, adding more concealer to hide the redness of her eyes, she had a long, long way to go in the recovery process. But now that she knew about the baby, it would have to start right now. She would have to put on the act of the century. She couldn't afford to show the smallest interest in what was going on between Serafina and him. He had made it clear that she had no right to ask such questions and she would have to respect that.

Had Cesare behaved badly? She thought he had. Scrapping the business-agreement-based marriage had been *his* idea, not hers. But honesty forced her to acknowledge that he had suggested at the time that they would have to see how well their marriage worked. In short, their marriage as such had been on a trial basis. And obviously, while it had worked incredibly well for Lizzie, it had not worked at all for Cesare. That hurt; that hurt her very much. It was a complete rejection of everything they had shared in and out of bed over the past month and it made her feel such an idiot for being so deliriously happy with him while failing utterly to notice that he did not feel the same way.

Lizzie went downstairs for breakfast, Archie at her heels. The instant the dog saw Cesare, who spoiled him shamelessly and taught him bad manners by feeding him titbits during meals, Archie hurried over to greet him. Cesare vaulted upright the minute she appeared. Unshaven, noticeably lacking his usual immaculate grooming, he still wore the same jeans and shirt. He raked a long-fingered brown hand through his tousled hair, looking effortlessly gorgeous but possibly less poised than he usually was.

'I won't lock the bedroom door again,' Lizzie promised, her heart-shaped face as still as a woodland pool. 'I'm sorry, I didn't think about what I was doing but the room's free now.'

'I'll get a shower before we leave for the airfield,' Cesare countered, his dark golden gaze scanning her expressionless face as if in search of something. 'Lizzie, we need to talk.'

Already having foreseen that he might feel that that was a necessity, Lizzie rushed to disabuse him of that dangerous notion. The very last thing she needed in her current shaky state of mind was a rehash of the breakdown of their relationship the night before. It wouldn't smooth over anything, wouldn't make her feel any better. How could it? Essentially he was dumping her and nothing he could say would ease that pain.

'That's the very last thing we need,' Lizzie told him briskly. 'All that needed to be said was said last night and we don't need to go over it again.'

'But—'

'What you said made sense to me when I thought it over,' Lizzie cut in, desperate to shut him up. 'This is business, nothing else. Let's stick to that from now on and I'll keep to my side of the bargain while your grandmother is staying with us on the island. I see no reason why we shouldn't bring this…er…project to a successful conclusion.'

Cesare blinked, disconcerted by the sound of such prosaic language falling from her lips. He was relieved that she was calm and grateful that she now intended to accompany him to Lionos for Athene's sake but he didn't agree with a single word she was saying. While, uniquely for him, he hesitated in a frantic inner search for the right approach to take with her, Lizzie took the wind out of his sails altogether.

'And that successful conclusion I mentioned?' Lizzie continued, a forced brightness of tone accompanying her wide fake smile. 'We're almost there because I'm pregnant.'

'Pregnant?' Cesare exclaimed in almost comical disbelief, springing back out of his seat again and yanking out the chair beside his own for her use. *'Madre di Dio…* sit down.'

Taken aback by his astonished reaction to her news, Lizzie sank down on the chair. 'It's not earth-shaking, Cesare. Women get pregnant every day.'

'You're my wife… It's a little more personal than that for me,' Cesare parried thickly, stepping behind her to rest his hands down on her slim, taut shoulders.

Alarmingly conscious of that physical contact, Lizzie froze in dismay. 'Could I ask you not to do that?'

'Do what?'

'Touch me,' she extended in an apologetic tone. 'I'll understand if you're forced to do it when your grandmother's around to make us look like a convincing couple but we're alone here and there's no need for it.'

Off-balanced by that blunt response, Cesare released her shoulders and backed away. He was thinking about the baby and he was fighting off an extraordinarily strong urge to touch her stomach, which he knew was weird, not to mention an urge destined to go unfulfilled.

'Forgive me,' he breathed abruptly. 'My immediate response was to touch you because I am full of joy about the baby.'

He had never looked *less* full of joy to Lizzie. In fact he looked a little pale and a lot tense, eyes shielded by his ridiculously long lashes, wide, sensual mouth compressed. She wanted to slap him so badly that her hands twitched on her lap. Like a magician pulling a white rabbit out of a hat, she had made her unexpected announcement, depending on it to wipe away the awkwardness lingering after their confrontation the night before. She had just let him know that he would never have a reason to touch her again *because* she had conceived. He should have been thrilled to be let off the hook when he didn't deserve it. Instead, however, a tense silence stretched like a rubber band threatening to snap.

'I didn't think it would happen so...*fast*,' Cesare admitted half under his breath.

'Well, it saves us a lot of hassle that it has,' Lizzie pronounced with as much positive emphasis as she could load into a single sentence. Hovering on the tip of her tongue was the highly inappropriate reminder that, after the amount of unprotected sex they had had, she thought it was more of a surprise that they hadn't hit the jackpot the first week.

'Hassle?'

'If we'd had to go for the artificial insemination, it might have been a bit...*icky*,' she mumbled, momentarily losing her grip on her relentless falsely cheerful front.

Icky, Cesare repeated inwardly. It was a pretty good description of how he was feeling. *Icky.* He had suffered a Damascene moment of revelation while he was with Serafina the previous night. A blinding light that even he could not ignore or sensibly explain away had shone over the events and emotions of the past month and he had finally understood how everything had gone so very wrong. Unfortunately for him, since Lizzie had joined him for breakfast, he had realised that 'wrong' was an understatement. He had dug a great big hole for himself and she was showing every intention of being perfectly happy to bury him alive in it.

Cesare went upstairs, ostensibly for a shower but he wanted privacy to make a phone call. In all his life he had never ever turned to Goffredo for advice but his father was the only touchy-feely male relative he had, who could be trusted to keep a confidence. His sisters were too young and out of the question. Each would discuss it with the other and then they would approach Lizzie to tell all because she was one of the sisterhood now and closer to his siblings than he was. Goffredo had one word of advice and it was an unpalatable one. Heaving a sigh, he then suggested his son imagine his life without her and take it from there. That mental exercise only exacerbated Cesare's dark mood.

Lizzie wore a floaty white cotton sundress to travel out to the island and took great pains with her hair and make-up. She knew that in the greater scheme of things her appearance was unimportant but was convinced that no woman confronted by a beauty like Serafina could remain indifferent to the possibility of unkind comparisons.

Close to running late for their flight, Cesare strode down the steps, a cool and sophisticated figure in beige chinos and an ivory cotton sweater that truly enhanced his bronzed skin tone and stunning dark eyes. Climbing into the car, he barely glanced at Lizzie and she knew all her fussing had been a pathetic waste of time.

Archie sat right in the middle of the back seat, halfway between them like a dog trying to work out how he could split himself into two parts. To Lizzie's intense annoyance, her pet ended up nudged up against a hard masculine thigh because Cesare was absently massaging Archie's ear, which reduced her dog to a pushover.

By the time they reached the airfield and boarded the helicopter, Lizzie was becoming increasingly frustrated. Cesare's brooding silence was getting to her and she wanted to know what was behind it. How could he simply switch off everything they had seemed to have together? It hadn't ever just been sex between them. There had been laughter and lots of talking and an intense sense of rightness as well. At least on *her* side, she conceded wretchedly.

His long, powerful thigh stretched as he shifted position and a heated ache blossomed between her thighs. That surge of hormonal chemistry mortified her. She reminded herself that that side of their marriage was over, she reminded herself that she was pregnant and she *still* ended up glancing back at that masculine thigh. Suddenly she was remembering that only the day before she would have stretched out a hand and stroked that hard male flesh, taking the initiative in a way that always surprised and pleased him. How had they seemed to be so attuned to each other when they so patently could not have been? Had she deceived herself? Had she dreamt up a whole fairy tale and tried to live it by putting Cesare in a starring role? Was this mess all her own wretched fault?

With such ideas torturing her and with a companion, who was almost as silent, it was little wonder that Lizzie had been airborne for over an hour when she was jolted by Cesare simply and suddenly turning round from the front passenger seat of the helicopter and urging her to look down at what he called *'her'* island.

'And Chrissie's,' she said unheard above the engine noise, stretching to peer over his broad shoulder as the craft dipped. She saw a long teardrop-shaped piece of land covered with lush green trees. '*That's* Lionos?' She gasped in astonishment for it was much bigger than she had expected. In her head she had cherished a not very inviting image of a rocky piece of land stuck in the middle of nowhere, for her mother had not made it sound an attractive place. At the same time their inheritance had never seemed very real to either her or her sister when they could not afford even to visit it.

Within minutes the helicopter was descending steeply to land in a clearing in the trees and for the first time in twenty-four hours a feeling of excited anticipation gripped Lizzie.

Ignoring Cesare's extended hand, she jumped down onto the ground and stared up at the white weatherboard house standing at the top of a slope. Like the island, it was bigger than she had expected.

'Athene told me that her father built it in the nineteen twenties and she had five siblings, so it had to be spacious,' Cesare supplied as he released Archie and the dog went scampering off to do what dogs did when they'd been confined for a long time. 'Primo says it really needs to be knocked down and rebuilt but he's done his best within the time frame he's had.'

'He's frighteningly efficient,' Lizzie remarked, mounting the slope, striving to ignore and avoid the supportive hand Cesare had planted to the base of her spine and a little breathless in her haste.

'Take it easy. It's hot and you're pregnant,' Cesare intoned.

'For goodness' sake!' Lizzie snapped. 'I'm only a tiny bit pregnant!'

In silence, Cesare rolled his eyes at that impossibility. He had all the consolation of knowing that he was reaping what he had sowed. Lizzie was not naturally either moody or short-tempered. In fact, in spite of her troubled childhood she had a remarkably cheerful nature, he conceded grimly. At least she had had a remarkably cheerful nature until he had contrived to destroy everything in what had to be an own goal of even more remarkable efficacy.

Primo greeted them at the front door and spread it wide. 'Workmen are still finishing off the utility area,' he admitted. 'But I believe the house is now presentable.'

Wide-eyed, Lizzie drifted through the tiled hall, which had been painted white, and moved on into a spacious reception room furnished with pieces that were an elegant mix of the traditional and the more contemporary. French windows draped with floral curtains opened out onto a terrace overlooking a secluded sandy cove. The view down the slope of a path through the trees to the beach was incredibly picturesque and unspoilt.

She walked through the house and as she peered into rooms some of her tension began to evaporate. In the wake of her mother's unappreciative descriptions, she was surprised to discover that it was actually a very attractive house and full of character. A room with a bathroom had been prepared for Athene's use on the ground floor. Lizzie mounted the stairs, which had wrought-iron ornamental balusters and a polished brass handrail. A bedroom had been sacrificed to provide en-suite bathrooms. Everywhere had been freshly decorated and kitted out, fabrics stirring softly in the breeze through open windows.

'What do you think?' Cesare asked from his stance on the landing.

'It's magical. I can understand why your grandmother never forgot this island. It must've been a wonderful house for kids,' she confided.

'Soon our child will follow that same tradition,' Cesare said gruffly.

'Well, possibly when he or she is visiting you. I won't be here as well,' Lizzie pointed out, quick to puncture that fantasy.

Cesare hovered in the strangest way, moving a step forward and then a step back, lashes suddenly lifting on strained dark golden eyes. 'And what if I wanted you to be here as well?'

'But you *wouldn't* want that,' Lizzie countered with unwelcome practicality. 'You will either have remarried or you'll have a girlfriend in tow.'

'What if I don't want that? What if I want you?' Cesare shot at her without warning, unnerved by that veiled reference to the divorce that would be required for his remarriage.

Lizzie lost colour, wondering what he was playing at, wondering if this was some new game on his terms. 'But you *don't*…want me, that is. You made that quite clear last night.'

'I *do* want you. I want to stay married,' Cesare bit out almost aggressively. 'Last night, you took me by surprise and I was confused. I made a mistake.'

Lizzie shook her pale head slowly and studied him in angry wonderment, temper stirring from the depths of the emotional turmoil she had been enduring since he had blown all her hopes and dreams to dust. 'I can't believe I'm hearing this. First you ask me for a business-based marriage, *then* you ask me to give our marriage a try and then you tell me we don't have a *real* marriage. As I see it, that's pretty comprehensive and not open to any other interpretation!'

She swivelled on her heel and deliberately walked past him to enter the room on the other side of the landing.

'I'm trying to say I'm sorry and you're not even listening!' Cesare growled from behind her.

'You can't apologise for what you feel…

neither of us can,' Lizzie parried curtly as she lodged by a window, hoping to look as though she were entranced by the view when in actuality all she could think about was escaping this agonising going-nowhere conversation with Cesare, who seemed not to have the first clue about how she might be feeling. 'I'm going to get changed and go off and explore.'

'Alone?' Cesare exclaimed.

'Yes. I like my own company. I had to—I worked alone for years,' she reminded him doggedly, walking past him on the landing, relieved when she saw the cases being carried upstairs into the master bedroom. 'I realise once Athene arrives tomorrow it'll be "game on" or whatever you want to call it... but could we...please not share a bedroom tonight?'

'Why are you not listening to anything I'm saying?' Cesare demanded in apparent disbelief. 'You won't even look at me!'

Lizzie had only felt free to look at him when he was *hers*. Now that he wasn't any more, she didn't want to fall victim to his essential gorgeousness all over again. Not looking was a form of self-defence, she reasoned wildly.

'Lizzie...' he breathed in a driven undertone.

Lizzie stiffened, tears prickling behind her wide eyes. 'I can't afford to listen to you. You upset me a lot last night and I really don't want to talk about that kind of stuff. It's pointless. I'm not really your wife. I may be living with you—'

'Expecting *my* child!' Cesare slotted in with greater force than seemed necessary.

'But you didn't choose to marry me because you cared about me, therefore it's not a proper marriage,' Lizzie replied as she reluctantly turned back to face him. 'And in your own immortal words everything else we've shared can be written off as "just sex".'

Cesare flinched at that reminder, his pallor below his bronzed skin palpable. 'I care about you *now*. I want to *keep* you.'

'I'm not a pet, Cesare...' Lizzie stared at him and frowned. 'Are you feeling all right? You know, you're acting very oddly.'

Goffredo's one-word piece of advice returned to haunt Cesare. 'I'm fine,' he said brusquely, lying through his teeth.

All of a quiver after that pointless exchange, her nerves jangling, Lizzie vanished into the bedroom, closed the door and opened her case to extract a sun top and shorts. She needed to blow the cobwebs off with a good walk. Cesare was nowhere to be seen when she went downstairs again and she went into the kitchen where Primo reigned supreme and eventually emerged with Primo's luxury version of a picnic meal and a bottle of water. With a little luck she could stay out until dark, then dive into bed and wake up to a new day and the big show for his poor grandmother's benefit.

Cesare was furious when he discovered that Lizzie had left the house. He strode down to the beach but there was no sign of her and not even a footprint on the pristine strand to suggest that she had come that way.

Several hours later, sunburned, foot weary and very tired after her jaunt across Lionos, Lizzie returned to discover that Cesare had gone out. Thankful, she settled down to supper as only Primo could make it. Sliding into her comfortable bed, she slept like a log.

Athene arrived mid-afternoon the next day. Cesare decided to be grateful for that because it brought Lizzie out of hiding. It had not once crossed his mind that she could be so intractable that she wouldn't even give him a hearing and then he thought of all the years she had slaved for her unappreciative and critical father and realised that she would have needed a strong, stubborn backbone.

Relaxed and colourful in a red sundress, Lizzie ushered Athene into her former childhood home. Tears shone in the old lady's eyes as she stood in the hall, gazing down the slope at the beautiful view. 'I thought it would all be overgrown and unrecognisable.'

'You showed me a photo once. I had the trees cut back,' Cesare told his grandmother softly. 'Shall I show you around?'

'Yes, this is your home and Lizzie's now,' Athene said a little tearfully and fumbled for a tissue. 'I have so many memories of my brothers and sisters here and now that they're all gone...'

Lizzie watched Cesare mop up his grandmother's tears with a deft touch and the right words and, minutes later, Athene was laughing as she recounted a childhood adventure with her brothers. She accompanied them on the official tour and Primo served afternoon tea out on the terrace, apparently an old tradition that Athene loved.

'Primo is an absolute treasure,' Athene told Lizzie as Cesare murmured an apology and withdrew to answer his phone before walking back into the house.

'And even better he *cooks*, which I'm not very good at,' Lizzie admitted, topping up the older woman's tea.

'Have you and Cesare had a row?' her companion asked without warning. 'I'm not an interfering old woman but I can feel that something's wrong.'

Lizzie felt that even an award-winning actress would have been challenged to carry off a smile at that point. 'A hiccup,' she downplayed studiously, her cheeks burning tomato-red as if the lie might be emblazoned on her forehead.

'My grandson has a remarkable brain, which serves him well in business. He's not quite so good at relationships,' Athene remarked wryly, gentle amusement in her warm brown eyes. 'There's bound to be hiccups as you call them. He's set in his ways and you'll challenge him. That's good for him. After all, anyone with eyes can see how deeply attached you are to each other.'

Lizzie's opinion of Athene's shrewdness nosedived at that pronouncement but the awkward moment passed over and she managed to relax again. The old lady eventually nodded off in the shade and Lizzie went back indoors.

'I need to warn you,' Lizzie almost whispered round the corner of the door of the room Cesare had set up as an office. 'Athene thinks we've had a row but that that's normal, so not really anything to worry about…but we'll need to make a real effort to impress.'

'Wouldn't it be easier simply to talk to me?' Cesare suggested, rising from behind his desk, all sleek Italian designer style in his tailored oatmeal-coloured casuals.

Lizzie continued to hover defensively in the doorway. 'I just don't think we have anything to talk about.'

'Do you know what time I went to bed last night?'

Lizzie blinked in confusion. 'How would I?'

'I was out tramping round the island looking for *you*. Primo couldn't raise a signal on my cell phone until midnight and I only found out then that you had returned to the house hours earlier!'

Lizzie dealt him an astonished look. 'But why were you looking for me in the first place? I wasn't lost.'

Cesare studied her as if she were irretrievably dim. 'There are all kinds of hazards out there. Fast currents in the sea, steep drops, dangerous rocks…'

Definitely behaving oddly, Lizzie labelled as she breathed in deep. 'Cesare, I'm not some little fluffy woman who can't look after herself. I'm an outdoors woman, used to working in all weathers and accustomed to constantly considering safety aspects on the farm.'

'But I was *worried* about you!' Cesare shot back at her in furious frustration.

Lizzie tossed her head, platinum-blonde hair shimmering across her slight shoulders in the sunlight, green eyes wide and wary. 'Well, you didn't need to be. I should've thought you would've been more worried about how Serafina is managing while we're together here when you belong with her.'

'I do not *belong* with Serafina!' Cesare raked at her so loudly, she jumped.

'No?'

'Do I strike you as being an idiot? I was a boy when I fell in love with her and full of romantic idealism but I'm all grown-up now,' he completed grimly.

'Well, you went rushing over to that *palazzo* fast enough the other night,' Lizzie argued in a less aggressive prompt. 'That *was* where you went, wasn't it?'

His stunning gaze widened to smouldering gold eyes of challenge. 'You think I went over there to *be* with her?'

'What else was I supposed to think?' Lizzie asked tightly. 'You left me in anger...'

'I wasn't angry with you, I was angry with *her*!' Cesare exclaimed in full-volume contradiction and Lizzie hastily backed to the door to close it firmly shut. 'How dare she have the insolence to approach my wife with the tacky details of an affair that happened a decade ago? I'd never heard such rubbish in my life and I was determined to finally have it out with her.'

Tacky details scarcely dovetailed with Serafina's suggestion that the barn episode had been a very precious memory for them both. Furthermore Lizzie was transfixed by the idea that he had rushed out of the house in a rage because Serafina had dared to approach his wife. Lizzie went pink over her misreading of the situation. 'And did you have it out with her?'

'*Sì*...I said a lot that she will not forget in a hurry. If she wasn't so vain, she would have accepted a long time ago that I would sooner chew off my own arm than have anything to do with her again. How could you think *that* of me?' Cesare raked at her in apparent wonderment. 'A woman who walked out on me because I wasn't rich enough? A disloyal, deceitful woman with the morals of a whore... She first offered herself back to me three years after she married Matteo and she did it again last night, which outraged me.'

Lizzie was so astonished by what she was finding out that she was rooted to the floor where she stood. Not only did he no longer care about Serafina, he evidently despised her and her eagerness to get him back. There was nothing fake about the driving derision he exuded. 'And of course you said no?'

'I never thought about her again after that first incident,' Cesare admitted flatly. 'By that stage I was grateful that, by marrying her, Matteo had saved me from making a serious mistake. No sane man would want a treacherous woman but, unfortunately for him, Matteo was besotted with her.'

Lizzie nodded slowly.

'Serafina won't be bothering either of us again, I assure you,' Cesare spelled out. 'She told me that she's bored with the countryside and will be moving back to her home in Florence.'

Lizzie was thinking about him having spent hours searching for her the night before because he was concerned that she might have met with an accident. Even though she was a seasoned outdoorswoman, she could not help but be touched by his naive assumption that she required his protection. She had made so many silly assumptions about Serafina and suddenly it was obvious that she had been listening to an extremely vain and spoilt woman spouting her belief that she was both irresistible and unforgettable. Cesare, on the other hand, had recovered from Serafina's betrayal by appreciating what a narrow escape he had had. That, she recognised, was absolutely in line with his character while rushing off to be with Serafina while he was married would not have been.

'I'm glad she's moving…I didn't like her,' Lizzie confided in a case of severe understatement. A light-headed sensation engulfed her and she gripped the back of a chair. 'Sorry, I get a bit dizzy now and again.'

'Is that like being only a tiny bit pregnant?' Cesare enquired, scooping her up as she swayed and planting her carefully down into the armchair. 'You need to be taking more rest and eating more food.'

'And what would you know about it?' Lizzie mumbled, momentarily giving way to the heaviness of her body and slumping into the depths of the chair like a sagging cushion.

'Possibly as much as you,' Cesare dared. 'I contacted an obstetrician for advice.'

Her lower lip dropped. 'You did…what?'

'It's my baby too,' he countered defensively. 'I had no idea how to look after you properly. It made sense to consult someone with the relevant knowledge.'

Her eyes stung again. Against all the odds, he was making such an effort to put across the point that, although he didn't want a real marriage with her, he did care about her welfare and their child's. Her throat convulsed. The tears she had been holding back were gaining on her, no matter how hard she tried to hold them back.

As Cesare stared across the barrier of his desk he saw two tears rolling down Lizzie's cheeks and his last defences fell to basement level. *He* had caused this fiasco. *He* had made her unhappy.

'I'm sorry…I'm *so* sorry,' Cesare told her gruffly.

Lizzie opened her wet eyes to find Cesare on his knees at her feet, stunning dark golden eyes stricken. 'Sorry? What about?'

'I'm sorry I hurt you. For years I had this set of rules with women,' he breathed raggedly, grabbing both her hands and crushing them between his. 'I never got involved. I never got involved with anyone after Serafina. And then I met you and I…I thought it would be the same with you and I tried to stick to the same rules but you were too much for me, only I didn't see it…'

'Slow down…' Lizzie begged, struggling to work out what he was telling her in such a rush. 'What are you saying?'

'That I'm mad about you, that I love you and I never want to lose you,' Cesare told her, crushing the life out of her poor fingers, his physical intensity as great as the emotional intensity now clear in his eyes.

Her lashes fluttered in bemusement. 'But you *said*—'

'Forget what I said. I was still trying to stick to my rules but it was idiocy,' he told her with a fierce fervour that was in itself impressive. 'I drove to Serafina's in a rage because she'd dared to try and upset you and I was driving back, thinking about what a vicious witch she is and thinking about you too…and that's when I realised.'

'That you love me?' Lizzie probed numbly, unsure what to believe, her thoughts spinning.

'I think I was scared to deal with what I was feeling for you, so I avoided thinking about it altogether…' Cesare hesitated. 'You know, I'm not much like Goffredo. I don't spend much time thinking about feelings and stuff.'

Lizzie was pleasantly surprised to learn that he had spent *any* time thinking about feelings but she couldn't smile when she was in shock. For the first time ever outside the bedroom she was seeing Cesare without the cool front he wore to the world and he wasn't half as smooth with words in the emotional category as he was with other things. Yet there was something hugely endearing about that inept surge of sentiment and confession because every syllable of it rang with raw honesty.

'So, you think you love me?' she pressed a little shakily, scared to hope, scared to dream, scared he didn't yet know his own heart.

'I *know* I love you. I only had to think of how warm and happy everything has seemed since we got married. I only have to think of being without you to know that what I feel for you is so much more than I ever felt for Serafina,' he confessed huskily.

A huge smile suddenly lit up Lizzie's face as she finally dared to really look at him again, scanning the superb bone structure, the straight nose and the perfect mouth. This time around, she revelled unashamedly in his essential gorgeousness because for the first time ever he felt like *hers*.

'I didn't want to fall for you either. Mum made so many mistakes and she was never really happy. I was afraid of falling for you,' Lizzie admitted, freeing a hand to brush his thick black hair off his brow in a gesture that came very close to an adoring caress. 'I really did think we were going to go the business route and then…my goodness, I couldn't stop thinking about you, couldn't take my eyes off you, couldn't keep my hands off you. You're sort of addictive but I didn't want to get hurt.'

'I hope I will never hurt you again.'

'Why are you still on your knees?' Lizzie whispered, genuinely bewildered.

'I rang my father for advice. I didn't give him *details*,' Cesare stressed when she looked at him in dismay. 'I just admitted that I'd said some very stupid things and he had only one word of advice…'

Lizzie viewed him expectantly.

Cesare bit the bullet and confided, *'Grovel.'*

'Seriously?' Lizzie giggled, tickled pink.

'I'm only going to do it once because I'm never ever likely to screw up as badly with you again, *amata mia*,' Cesare delivered, springing back upright without any loss of presence to open the door before striding back to scoop his wife up out of her chair. 'I've learned a lot from this experience.'

'Have you?' Lizzie asked curiously, resting back against his broad chest, sublimely happy just to be in his arms again, breathing in the delicious scent of him and free to think about all the wicked bedroom skills he was undoubtedly about to unleash on her.

'For a whole month I took you for granted. I'll never make that mistake again. I love you. My family loves you.'

'Even my father said that you were a sensible man,' Lizzie inputted with amusement.

'Very sensible. You're a wonderful woman, *cara mia.'* Cesare lowered her the whole formidable length of his lean, hard body to the landing floor and kissed her with hungry, driving passion.

Lizzie was more than ready to drown now in his potent fervour to reconnect with her. Excitement laced her happiness with a heady sense of joy and quiet security. She simply knew that she had a glorious life ahead of her with her husband and her child.

On the ground floor, Athene was in a self-congratulating mood.

'I do hope I've sorted them out. Cesare's stubborn but his wife is soft. As if I would simply fall asleep in the middle of a conversation!' Athene chuckled as she took over Primo's kitchen to make her grandson's favourite cake. 'I think we'll have a rather late dinner tonight, Primo…'

Three years later, Lizzie relaxed on the front veranda of the house on Lionos while she awaited Cesare's return from a business trip. Her children were with her. Max was two, a toddler with the unusual combination of his mother's pale hair and his father's dark eyes. He was industriously racing toy cars on the boards beneath her feet and making very noisy vroom-vroom sounds. In a travel cot in the shade a dark-haired six-month-old baby girl slumbered, sucking her thumb, while Archie dozed on the front doormat.

Gianna had not been planned, Lizzie reflected, her eyes tender as she bent down to try and extract her daughter's thumb from her rosebud mouth. She managed it but even in sleep within minutes the thumb crept back. She gave up when she heard the distant beat of the helicopter's approach, sliding upright to get a better view over the bay.

Max abandoned his cars and joined her. 'Papa...Papa!' he exclaimed, well aware of what that sound presaged in his secure little world.

Lizzie stroked her son's silky head and smiled dreamily. She always enjoyed the sunshine and the peace on Lionos but it would soon be disrupted by Cesare's forceful, exciting presence and she couldn't wait; she really couldn't wait. Three years had not dimmed the chemistry between them.

Athene spent spring to summer on the island, preferring her Rome apartment and its greater convenience in the winter. Lizzie had grown to love her husband's grandmother as much as she loved the rest of his family. He had been so blessed by all that love and warmth and to give him his due becoming a parent had made Cesare more sensitive towards his own relatives. He was much more relaxed with his large and convivial family than he had once been and his father and his sisters were frequent visitors to their homes in London, Tuscany and Lionos. Lizzie often teased her husband that she had stayed married to him because she couldn't bear the thought of losing his family.

Sadly, since her marriage she had seen much less of her own father and sister. Brian Whitaker came on occasional visits but he didn't like flying or foreign food or even people talking their own language in his vicinity. Lizzie had purchased a compact home for the older man in the village where he had grown up and he seemed as happy there as he would be anywhere. She had taken him to see a consultant for his Parkinson's disease and he was on a new drug regimen and showing considerable improvement.

Disconcertingly, although Chrissie regularly hitched a flight home with Cesare when he was in London on business, she had become fiercely independent and now had secrets she was reluctant to share. Lizzie had watched anxiously from the sidelines of her sister's life as things went badly wrong for the sibling she adored and troubled times rolled in. Cesare had advised her to let Chrissie stand on her own feet and not to interfere when Lizzie would more happily have rushed in and tried to wave a magic wand over Chrissie's difficulties to make them vanish. She had had to accept that Chrissie was an adult with the right to make her own decisions... and her own mistakes. That said, however, she was still very close to her sister and very protective of her.

The helicopter finally appeared in the bright blue cloudless sky and descended out of sight behind the trees. Max was jumping up and down by that stage and clapping his hands. In a flash he was gone and running down the slope to greet his father with Archie chasing at his heels, shaggy ears flying, tongue hanging out.

'Go ahead,' a voice said softly from behind Lizzie. 'I'll sit with Gianna.'

Lizzie flashed a grateful smile at Athene and raced down the slope after her son like a teenager. Cesare took one look at his wife, pale hair flying, cheeks flushed below brilliant green eyes full of warmth and welcome, and set Max down again to open his arms.

'I really missed you!' Lizzie complained into his shoulder. 'You're far too missable.'

'I'll work on it,' Cesare promised, smoothing her hair back from her brow, wondering whether or not he should admit that he had worked night and day to get back to her within a week. He missed his family more every time he left them behind and planned complex travel schedules that minimised his absences.

'I shouldn't be whingeing,' Lizzie muttered guiltily, drinking in the familiar musky scent of his skin, her body quickening with the piercingly sweet pleasure-pain of desire that made her slim body quiver against his long, lean length.

'It's not whingeing. You missed me...I missed you, *amata mia*,' Cesare said huskily. 'We are so lucky to have found each other.'

They walked slowly back up the slope, Max swiftly overtaking them, Archie lagging behind. Cesare stilled to turn Lizzie round and curve loving hands to her cheeks to gaze down at the face he never tired of studying. 'I'm crazy about you, Signora Sabatino.'

'And me...about you.' Beaming in the sunshine, Lizzie linked her arms round his neck and tilted her head back invitingly.

She slid into that kiss like melting ice cream, honeyed languor assailing her in the safe circle of his arms. Cesare was home and a rainbow burst of happiness made her feel positively buoyant.

* * * * *

LARGER-PRINT BOOKS!
GET 2 FREE LARGER-PRINT NOVELS PLUS
2 FREE GIFTS!

H HARLEQUIN®

INTRIGUE®

BREATHTAKING ROMANTIC SUSPENSE

YES! Please send me 2 FREE LARGER-PRINT Harlequin Intrigue® novels and my 2 FREE gifts (gifts are worth about $10). After receiving them, if I don't wish to receive any more books, I can return the shipping statement marked "cancel." If I don't cancel, I will receive 6 brand-new novels every month and be billed just $5.49 per book in the U.S. or $5.99 per book in Canada. That's a saving of at least 13% off the cover price! It's quite a bargain! Shipping and handling is just 50¢ per book in the U.S. and 75¢ per book in Canada.* I understand that accepting the 2 free books and gifts places me under no obligation to buy anything. I can always return a shipment and cancel at any time. Even if I never buy another book, the two free books and gifts are mine to keep forever.

199/399 HDN F42Y

Name _____ (PLEASE PRINT) _____

Address _____ Apt. # _____

City _____ State/Prov. _____ Zip/Postal Code _____

Signature (if under 18, a parent or guardian must sign)

Mail to the **Harlequin® Reader Service:**
IN U.S.A.: P.O. Box 1867, Buffalo, NY 14240-1867
IN CANADA: P.O. Box 609, Fort Erie, Ontario L2A 5X3

**Are you a subscriber to Harlequin Intrigue books
and want to receive the larger-print edition?
Call 1-800-873-8635 today or visit www.ReaderService.com.**

* Terms and prices subject to change without notice. Prices do not include applicable taxes. Sales tax applicable in N.Y. Canadian residents will be charged applicable taxes. Offer not valid in Quebec. This offer is limited to one order per household. Not valid for current subscribers to Harlequin Intrigue Larger-Print books. All orders subject to credit approval. Credit or debit balances in a customer's account(s) may be offset by any other outstanding balance owed by or to the customer. Please allow 4 to 6 weeks for delivery. Offer available while quantities last.

Your Privacy—The Harlequin® Reader Service is committed to protecting your privacy. Our Privacy Policy is available online at www.ReaderService.com or upon request from the Harlequin Reader Service.

We make a portion of our mailing list available to reputable third parties that offer products we believe may interest you. If you prefer that we not exchange your name with third parties, or if you wish to clarify or modify your communication preferences, please visit us at www.ReaderService.com/consumerschoice or write to us at Harlequin Reader Service Preference Service, P.O. Box 9062, Buffalo, NY 14269. Include your complete name and address.

HILPI3R

LARGER-PRINT BOOKS!

GET 2 FREE LARGER-PRINT NOVELS PLUS

2 FREE GIFTS!

⊞ HARLEQUIN®

Romance

From the Heart, For the Heart

YES! Please send me 2 FREE LARGER-PRINT Harlequin® Romance novels and my 2 FREE gifts (gifts are worth about $10). After receiving them, if I don't wish to receive any more books, I can return the shipping statement marked "cancel." If I don't cancel, I will receive 4 brand-new novels every month and be billed just $4.84 per book in the U.S. or $5.24 per book in Canada. That's a savings of at least 19% off the cover price! It's quite a bargain! Shipping and handling is just 50¢ per book in the U.S. and 75¢ per book in Canada.* I understand that accepting the 2 free books and gifts places me under no obligation to buy anything. I can always return a shipment and cancel at any time. Even if I never buy another book, the two free books and gifts are mine to keep forever.

119/319 HDN F43Y

Name _____ (PLEASE PRINT) _____

Address _____ Apt. # _____

City _____ State/Prov. _____ Zip/Postal Code _____

Signature (if under 18, a parent or guardian must sign)

Mail to the **Harlequin® Reader Service:**
IN U.S.A.: P.O. Box 1867, Buffalo, NY 14240-1867
IN CANADA: P.O. Box 609, Fort Erie, Ontario L2A 5X3

Want to try two free books from another line?
Call 1-800-873-8635 or visit www.ReaderService.com.

* Terms and prices subject to change without notice. Prices do not include applicable taxes. Sales tax applicable in N.Y. Canadian residents will be charged applicable taxes. Offer not valid in Quebec. This offer is limited to one order per household. Not valid for current subscribers to Harlequin Romance Larger-Print books. All orders subject to credit approval. Credit or debit balances in a customer's account(s) may be offset by any other outstanding balance owed by or to the customer. Please allow 4 to 6 weeks for delivery. Offer available while quantities last.

Your Privacy—The Harlequin® Reader Service is committed to protecting your privacy. Our Privacy Policy is available online at www.ReaderService.com or upon request from the Harlequin Reader Service.

We make a portion of our mailing list available to reputable third parties that offer products we believe may interest you. If you prefer that we not exchange your name with third parties, or if you wish to clarify or modify your communication preferences, please visit us at www.ReaderService.com/consumerschoice or write to us at Harlequin Reader Service Preference Service, P.O. Box 9062, Buffalo, NY 14269. Include your complete name and address.

HRLP13R

LARGER-PRINT BOOKS!
GET 2 FREE LARGER-PRINT NOVELS PLUS
2 FREE GIFTS!

◆ HARLEQUIN®

super romance®

More Story...More Romance

YES! Please send me 2 FREE LARGER-PRINT Harlequin® Superromance® novels and my 2 FREE gifts (gifts are worth about $10). After receiving them, if I don't wish to receive any more books, I can return the shipping statement marked "cancel." If I don't cancel, I will receive 6 brand-new novels every month and be billed just $5.69 per book in the U.S. or $5.99 per book in Canada. That's a savings of at least 16% off the cover price! It's quite a bargain! Shipping and handling is just 50¢ per book in the U.S. or 75¢ per book in Canada.* I understand that accepting the 2 free books and gifts places me under no obligation to buy anything. I can always return a shipment and cancel at any time. Even if I never buy another book, the two free books and gifts are mine to keep forever.

139/339 HDN F46Y

Name	(PLEASE PRINT)

Address	Apt. #

City	State/Prov.	Zip/Postal Code

Signature (if under 18, a parent or guardian must sign)

Mail to the **Harlequin® Reader Service:**
IN U.S.A.: P.O. Box 1867, Buffalo, NY 14240-1867
IN CANADA: P.O. Box 609, Fort Erie, Ontario L2A 5X3

Are you a current subscriber to Harlequin Superromance books and want to receive the larger-print edition?
Call 1-800-873-8635 today or visit www.ReaderService.com.

* Terms and prices subject to change without notice. Prices do not include applicable taxes. Sales tax applicable in N.Y. Canadian residents will be charged applicable taxes. Offer not valid in Quebec. This offer is limited to one order per household. Not valid for current subscribers to Harlequin Superromance Larger-Print books. All orders subject to credit approval. Credit or debit balances in a customer's account(s) may be offset by any other outstanding balance owed by or to the customer. Please allow 4 to 6 weeks for delivery. Offer available while quantities last.

Your Privacy—The Harlequin® Reader Service is committed to protecting your privacy. Our Privacy Policy is available online at www.ReaderService.com or upon request from the Harlequin Reader Service.

We make a portion of our mailing list available to reputable third parties that offer products we believe may interest you. If you prefer that we not exchange your name with third parties, or if you wish to clarify or modify your communication preferences, please visit us at www.ReaderService.com/consumerschoice or write to us at Harlequin Reader Service Preference Service, P.O. Box 9062, Buffalo, NY 14269. Include your complete name and address.

HSRLP13R